Ransom Seaborn

BILL DEASY

yelluminous

Published by Velluminous Press
www.velluminous.com

ISBN-13: 978-1-905605-08-8
ISBN-10: 1-905605-08-0

cover illustration by Elspeth Fahey

Ransom Seaborn

for
Holden

The shower water felt like tiny pebbles on my skin. It had been days, maybe even a week. I put on fresh jeans and a t-shirt, and set up shop at this worn, nicked, underused desk. PowerBook, 20 ounce Styrofoam coffee cup, ashtray, cigarettes—all the essentials.

It's raining outside, a fine mist. I hear it just barely against the window—imaginary childhood horses rushing toward me from beyond the pale. I'm trying not to think too much about what I'm writing...what I'm doing here. I guess I have a story to tell you.

Here goes nothing.

Chapter One

A tweed oval rug covered the center of the black-speckled dark green floor. Three pairs of shiny dress shoes were placed neatly beneath one of the two single beds. The corner desk was blottered, calendered and armed for academic warfare. A framed and autographed picture of George Bush sat atop a nearby dresser.

When the letter came informing me that I would be living in Jefferson, a dormitory normally reserved for juniors and seniors, I didn't question my good fortune. How perfect, I thought, to have freshman orientation—two full days—to ease into my new environment without the distraction of the swarming masses. My visions of isolated grandeur were shattered when we discovered room 223 already inhabited.

"Looks like your roommate's already moved in, Dan," said my mother, who has a flair for stating the obvious.

At that moment we heard the sound of a toilet flushing, a faucet running, a door opening, and loud, slow footsteps squeaking down the hall. Time stood still as we awaited the author of the steps.

"Hi there," he said when he finally appeared in the doorway making the face I later learned was his smile. "My name's Matt Price. Hope you don't mind. I took the liberty of claiming the far bed."

"Hi, Matt," my parents replied, too quickly, too enthusiastically, extending their hands and offering introductions.

"Dan Finbar," I said when my turn came, "but people call me Fin, or Finbar."

For as long as I could remember that was how I had introduced myself. It was rare that anyone outside my family called me by my first name. My little sister, Sara, chuckled. She did that a lot.

"Do you play?" Matt asked formally, pointing at the battered, black guitar case I still held in my left hand.

"No, Matt, I just carry this around to stay pumped," is what my snide alter ego said in my head—an unspoken jab made all the more biting for the lack of musculature on my slight frame.

"Yeah," I replied.

"I play trumpet," he offered, his braces glinting in the afternoon sun. Did he think we would jam? Was he picturing wild Muppet-like impromptu trumpet-guitar concerts on lazy Sunday afternoons? I couldn't help staring at him. He looked like a marionette chiseled from dried mud; a claymation figure—what's-his-name—the elf who wanted to be a dentist. He wore stiff, navy blue jeans, a short-sleeved brown and white-checkered shirt and dark brown Docksiders. It appeared as though the entire ensemble, and him along with it, had been dry cleaned recently, heavy starch. His flat face bore wire-rimmed glasses and a pained expression beneath brown crew cut hair.

"I'm in the ROTC," he explained as we headed for the stairs. "We had to come a week early for drills and stuff."

His voice possessed a nasally timbre; a distinct, whiny quality.

"What's the ROTC?" I asked.

"Reserve Officers' Training Corps. It means the military pays my way, and they get four years of my life when I graduate."

"A military man," my father observed too cheerfully. "Where are you from, Matt?"

"A rinky-dink little town called Dillsburgh, just outside of Harrisburg. I'm sure you've never heard of it."

Sara mouthed the words "rinky-dink" and bit her lower lip to keep from laughing as the five of us emerged from Jefferson. We transferred the rest of my belongings from the car to the room in one trip, then Matt directed us to the gymnasium in the center of Alumni Hall where an opening convocation was scheduled.

❦

The basketball hoops had been ratcheted up and a makeshift stage assembled in front of the locker room doors. The maple bleachers and fold out chairs, which covered the court, were filled nearly to capacity. My parents, Sara and I found an empty space at the top of the stands.

After a heart-felt prayer from Reverend Jones, President Jonathon Phillips towered before us.

"Welcome parents, brothers, sisters, friends and, most importantly, you new bright lights of Harrison College," he bellowed across the pin-drop silent auditorium, a balding bear of a man, a physical and intellectual giant. "It is with great excitement and eager anticipation that I stand here this afternoon and urge you, urge all of you, parents and children alike, to prepare for change—the changing circumstances which result from technology and innovation in our lives."

As our esteemed leader proceeded to discuss the invention of electricity and the deep, social transformation it brought about, I stared around at my empty-eyed classmates and their sad, hopeful parents, all gazing forward, expectantly searching the air for a behavioral blueprint, an easy-to-follow guide to letting go, moving on.

"Our faith in Christ is constant and eternal," Dr. Phillips finally summarized, his voice rising in fervent exclamation. "It doesn't change with scientific discoveries or technological advances. It is there as our foundation in this age and in ages to come. It is the bedrock for our college and our lives."

The applause was deafening. I sat motionless, a Catholic fish in deep, Presbyterian water. (Did I mention that Harrison is a shining bastion of free-market economics and good old white-sleeved Christian fundamentalism? My parents were both liberal leaning Catholics. I'm still not sure how I wound up there.)

Afterwards, following a late lunch at McDonald's, which Sara spent pinching her nose and practicing her Matt Price imitation, a strange silence filled my head. I struggled to conceal my dread when my teary mother hugged me and wished me well. My father shook my hand firmly, nearly pulling my arm from its socket.

"We love you, Dan," he said, meeting my eyes with his own, trying to reassure me. "You're gonna be fine."

"Make sure you talk to people," my mom added, as she wound down the passenger-side window and blew me a kiss.

"Come home soon," Sara called. "But not too soon."

I smiled back weakly. A dull ache spread through my suddenly shallow chest cavity as I stood on the sidewalk watching them begin their drive back to Pittsburgh.

Late that night, after a cookout on the soccer field and a 'Welcome Freshmen' party in the crepe-papered intramural room, I lay awake on my rickety new bed staring at the ceiling. Laughter trickled in through the open window. The lifelong home in which I'd awoken that morning was now a lost, distant continent. I fell asleep slowly to the sound of Matt Price's whistling nose.

❦

Day two of orientation was filled with more forced socialization. Between the chaotic soccer free-for-all and the late-day picnic, I managed to steal some alone time and explore the well-kept Harrison grounds. Following cement pathways through the interlacing rectangles that made up the campus, I breathed in the rarefied country air and familiarized myself with the spaces among and around the school buildings.

My thoughts flickered between my old and new worlds. Memories of the past twenty four hours, the longest of my life, mingled with still-fresh images from last week's string of good-bye parties, an entire summer of drunken revelry. And there were other memories, too, older ones, of the childhood that had ended. My mother holding my small boy-hand as we walked the beach in New Jersey. ("Each squeeze is a word," she'd explained gently. "I—LOVE—YOU.") Lazy, after-school sitcoms we'd all seen at least twice. My brother, three sisters and I seated along with our parents at the dinner table, our hands joined in mumbled prayer. The life that was forever beyond my backwards reach.

❦

The first day of classes found me standing beneath the Underhill Hall clock collecting my bearings amid a torrent of students, all of whom seemed to know where they were going. Plastic plaques engraved with room numbers hung in neat rectangles above each door. I followed their trail to 112, Literature 101. Dr. Julia Mabry greeted us with a gentle smile and a nervous laugh.

"Many of you are freshmen," she began. "Welcome to Harrison."

Introduction to Government came next. It was taught by the adorable, if somewhat unintelligible, Ray Rider with his buzz cut and signature quote, "I can feel for you but I can't quite reach you." He passed out copies of the course syllabus and proceeded to spin a web of unconnected anecdotes.

Creative Writing concluded my first day of classes. Dr. William Exley, the only communist on the faculty, ambled among us, wild-eyed and eager to offend.

"Can anyone tell me what good writing is?" he began. Our silence goaded him. "Come on, I presume you all have the ability to speak. What is good writing?"

Still nothing. He perched on the edge of his desk and pulled a folded sheet of paper from his shirt pocket. It was a letter he had received that morning from a former student.

"I had him back in Harrison's heyday," he joked, "before the administration had so successfully purged the campus of personality. I always knew he was special." He enunciated his words in such a way that everything he said could be construed as sarcasm. "Now he's a novelist, if you can believe that," he continued. "And a damn fine one I might add. See what you all can accomplish if you'll only follow my simple instructions?"

He put on his glasses and speed-muttered the first few paragraphs to himself until he came to the portion he wanted to share with us, dramatically clearing his throat before quoting:

What have I learned about love, you ask. Only that it's a very hard game to master, and luck has a lot to do with the outcome.

Though I've been married and divorced, I understand next to nothing about love.

But no, I take that back. I have learned a couple of things from Stephanie, the woman with whom I have enjoyed, for the past three years, a relationship more satisfying than my marriage was. Before we moved in together, I had thought myself much better at divorce than marriage (my ex-wife and I must have set a record for efficiency and swiftness), but now it becomes clear that I would have been good at marriage if I'd chosen a compatible partner. That's one thing I've learned.

The second thing is that there are three major stages to any love affair, as there are to most of life's processes, I suspect: the preamble, the mainbody, and the end. The reason love makes clowns out of so many of us, and brings so many of us to grief, is that parts one and two are so dissimilar. I'm talking about the heart-stopping thrill of falling in love, as opposed to the placid, satisfied existence enduring love settles into. What's the connection? How can one possibly understand the peacefulness of floating down a slow stream in a canoe when one's only experience with water has been going over the falls?

He shoved the wrinkled paper back into his front pocket, a satisfied grin on his face. "Now, that is good writing," he exclaimed. "God, I love good writing."

He concluded the class that morning by saying, "Just write brilliantly," and urging us to go familiarize ourselves with the library. Rather than risk a conversation over lunch, I did as he suggested and headed for the stacks.

🍁

The Charles Pavlick Memorial Library was located in front of the computer center and stood parallel with my dorm, though separated by a football field-sized lawn. I entered through the rear and was assaulted instantly by mugginess. Students anxious to get a jump on their work would do so at the risk of heat stroke.

I went through the front lobby, past the check out and information desks, and turned left down the wide center aisle. Sunlight streamed through a row of high, rectangular windows on the south wall, giving the space a dusty, heavenly appearance. The carpeted main room was unoccupied and stood in stark contrast to the metallic, two-story sidecar section that housed the majority of the books. I walked among the stacks perusing titles, noticing an abundance of religious and political texts. Finally, upstairs, I found the meager collection of fiction. I scanned the rows until finding the works of J.D. Salinger. Two years earlier, while still nestled in the heart of high school in Pittsburgh, I read *The Catcher in the Rye* for the first time. It became the language of our small group in Senior English, often quoted and openly revered. It stood now as a symbol of lost security. I retrieved a copy and sat down at the nearest desk.

When I looked up, I noticed a thin, wiry student writing furiously at the table to my right. His left hand supported his tilting head, fingers buried in the disheveled black strands. He wore faded jeans, a faded black t-shirt and faded black boots. His flexed left biceps gave his writing the appearance of an athletic activity. He glanced in my direction and I returned my attention to the world of Holden Caulfield's New York City.

❧

As high-noon yellow gave way to mellow, late-day blue, I entered my dorm and climbed the stairs to the second floor. Inserting my key into the door lock, I noticed the mad writer from the library doing the same two doors down. An unlit cigarette dangled from his closed mouth and a brown notebook was tucked under his left arm. Again I stared and again he caught me, before disappearing into his room.

❦

Matt Price's loud entrance awakened me. He stood for an instant in the doorway's rectangular coffin of light before flipping the switch and rousing me for certain.

"Hi," he droned, seeming not to notice that I'd been sleeping. "You know why they called it Jefferson?"

Matt was in the habit of imparting Harrison trivia whenever the mood hit. Learning the history of our college was an integral part of his ROTC training, and he liked to spread the informational wealth.

"No," I answered, raising myself into a seated position. "Why did they call it Jefferson, Matt?"

"Herbert Jefferson, class of '49," he spouted. "He was this, like, world famous laissez-faire economist…gave Harrison scads of money."

I allowed a moment to give the appearance of digesting this startling new information then asked, "What's the deal with the guy in 219?"

"Ransom Seaborn," he replied.

"You know him?" I followed. "What's his name again? Ransom Seaborn?"

"Ransom Seaborn," he repeated as if he couldn't believe it himself. "No one knows him. He's, like, this mystery man who doesn't talk to anyone. If you say 'Hi' to him he acts like you're not even there." Matt's voice began to pitch up. He was visibly enlivened by this visit to the rumor mill. "I don't know. I didn't hear this first hand, obviously, but a friend of mine said he killed someone when he was in high school and his parents sent him here to straighten him out."

"He a junior?" I asked, not quite able to digest the whole murderer-next-door thing.

"Yeah," he replied. "He has the only single in the building." Matt removed the sweater he had worn to his afternoon class and replaced it with another, à la Mister Rogers.

"You wanna go to dinner over at Block?" he asked. Of the two cafeterias on campus, Block tended to draw the upper-classmen.

"Yeah," I replied, thinking if I played my cards right I might not meet another freshman all year. Who knew? Maybe some day I'd be the murderer next door.

※

Matt went to see "American Graffiti" in the Lawford Auditorium that night so I had the room to myself. I called home and assured my parents I was doing fine then took a run on my first batch of homework. By ten o'clock, I'd had enough. I grabbed my worn copy of *Franny and Zooey* and headed off in the direction of the Student Union, known for some reason as 'The Podunk.' Ransom Seaborn emerged from his room as I approached it and couldn't help noticing me.

"Well, if it isn't the staring man," he said dryly. "And a Salinger fan, to boot," he added, noticing my book.

"You read it?" I asked, hearing my voice sounding cool and detached, even as my pulse quickened.

"Lord Jesus Christ have mercy on my soul," he answered, quoting the mantra Franny repeats to herself in the story, then continued by me in the opposite direction.

※

I spent the night reading and roaming the campus. Standing at the bottom of the main quadrangle, I stared up at the clock illuminated atop Rockwell, the science building. A busload of students returning from an off-campus party unloaded noisily at the entrance to the college. Their voices rose and fell, as though unified, and moved closer through the night. I stood still, an invisible, human arrow, dividing them as they passed.

I recognized some of them as fellow freshmen and wondered how they had managed to assimilate so easily. I seemed always stuck on the precipice between self-doubt and excitement, a state that rendered me useless, socially speaking (and often still does). I was the lonely boy clinging to the belief that the party would one day be magically delivered to his doorstep.

🍁

Among the many confounding policies of Harrison College was the existence of Saturday classes. Accounting 101, the course that would forever save the business world from my presence, met bright and early the next morning. My alarm clock sounded at 7:45 and I shuffled sleepily down the hallway to the communal bathroom. As I passed room 219, I heard the soft strands of a familiar Van Morrison song, *Into the Mystic*. I was briefly transported back to a hundred overcast afternoons, lying on my bed, listening to my brother's records, discovering music.

Entering yet another cloudless day, I covered the short distance between Jefferson and Lawford, determined to befriend the quiet guy with the strange name. Ransom Seaborn.

Opportunity knocked quickly. After leaving class, I decided to swallow my fears and go alone to the cafeteria for breakfast after days of eating peanut butter and jelly in my room. I pushed my plastic tray along the metal conveyor, then scanned the room for a place to park.

Ransom sat alone in the far corner. I passed the rows of half-filled tables, turned down the last aisle, and took the seat across from him.

"I heard Van Morrison coming from your room this morning," I ventured. "I love that album."

No reply. His mouth was full.

"Ever heard *Astral Weeks?*" I asked.

Still nothing. I persevered.

"I saw Van Morrison last summer at the Merriwether Post Pavilion in Maryland. It was amazing. He did a ten minute version of *Sweet Thing.*" Finally he looked up at me. "I couldn't believe it," I continued. "I almost had a heart attack."

"I have heard *Astral Weeks,*" he said.

Although I already knew his name, I thought the possibility of our friendship might be made official if he told me himself so I said, "My name's Dan Finbar. Most people call me Fin."

"Ransom Seaborn," he replied faintly. "See you round, Fin."

He lifted his tray and carried it to the dishwashers' window. Not a clear victory, but I'd take it.

❧

Much of my free time was spent browsing the freshman directory and falling in love with various female strangers. Their 1 inch by 1 inch black and white faces smiled up at me, instilling hope. It never occurred to me that I would have to actually speak to one of them in order to begin any kind of emotional or physical interaction. I imagined it all just kind of happening one day by chance, when they finally saw the light and heard me singing and playing my guitar as they walked along the sidewalk beneath my second story window.

"Hello up there," they would yell between nervous giggles. "I don't mean to be forward—or maybe I do—but do you think I could come up to your room and introduce myself?"

"Come on up," I would say offhandedly, the very model of enigmatic detachment. (This, of course, hearkens back to that party-at-my-doorstep thing.)

And so it was that first Saturday night. I passed the time leafing through the directory between heart-rending musical outpourings beside the open window. Following a particularly powerful reading of my latest composition, I halted my unattended concert to go relieve myself.

Ransom stood at the far sink scrubbing a spot on his shirt. I walked over to the urinal and went about my business, playing it cool.

"That you singing?" he asked my image in the mirror.

"Yeah," I replied, staring at the wall, embarrassed by how loud I must have been but hearing no annoyance in the inquiry.

"So you're into Salinger," he continued—his voice thick and sugary. "Have you ever read his short stories?"

"Yeah," I replied, washing my hands in the basin two over from his.

"I like that one, *A Perfect Day For Banana Fish.* Remember that?" he asked as he opened the door and waited for me to walk out in front of him. I smelled the alcohol on his breath as I passed.

"Drinking is forbidden here, you know," I said with mock severity. "I could have you thrown out for this."

"You wouldn't do that," he assured me in an exaggerated whisper as we moved down the hall. "You like J.D. Salinger. Care for a cocktail, Finbar?"

"Sure," I replied, stunned by the invitation, and followed him as he opened and entered his room.

It looked like a monk lived there. Two photographs, indistinguishable in the near darkness and pasted to the wall above the head of his unmade bed, were the only signs of personality. Nick Drake sang from the windowsill and cigarette smoke wafted through the stale air. I pulled the chair out from under his candle-lit desk as he lifted a half-filled gallon jug of Mad Dog 20/20 from the closet.

"I do remember *Banana Fish*," I said. "That's the one about the guy who talks with that little girl in the ocean then goes and kills himself, right? I think my favorite is *The Laughing Man*, though. Do you remember it, about the guy who tells the kids that story?"

He didn't answer. He handed me a cafeteria glass filled with the cheap red wine, then took a seat on the bed. The first sip warmed my blood.

"Where're you from?" I asked.

"Hanover, New Hampshire," he replied, lighting his next cigarette with the butt of his last one. "Live free or die."

"I have a friend who worked at a camp near there last summer. I can't remember the name."

"There are hundreds of camps around there," he explained. "Parents send their kids away to get sunburned and socialized, among other things."

Smoke streamed from his mouth and nostrils. He flicked his ash into an empty Coke can. The angles of his face—his jaws, his cheeks—were so severe it almost looked like he was wearing stage make-up. Hamlet of Hanover.

"Something with the word 'moose' in it, I think," I said. "How'd you end up here?"

"A friend of my dad's came here a long time ago. My dad thought it might have a calming effect on me."

I recalled the theory Matt had shared. Ransom seemed to read my mind. "What'd you hear?" he asked. "That I killed a kid in high school or that I was a star witness in a big Mafia trial? Or is there a new story floating around?"

"Killed a kid in high school," I confessed.

"Not true. Sorry to disappoint you. I was tempted a few times."

My fourth glass of Mad Dog found us engaged in a heated debate over the meaning of a Van Morrison song, *Madame George.*

"It's about a drag queen," he insisted, now flagrantly inebriated.

"No way," I countered. "It's about a heroin addict. I read it somewhere." We played the song over and over and paused the disc on lines particularly crucial to our arguments.

When we finished the bottle, Ransom suggested we walk into Pembrook to buy cigars. Stone steps guided us away from the halls of academe, towards the quaint, small town of Pembrook, Pennsylvania. The firmament loomed clear and dazzling overhead. I wondered aloud if clouds even existed in this strip of Pennsylvania sky. Maybe God wanted Harrison to remain in a constant state of atmospheric stability, so as not to distract his children from their heavenly endeavors.

I was drunk.

"I have to take a piss," Ransom said, and we stopped to water the parched earth of the short-cut path to Main Street.

Standing there, pecker in hand, I stared up at the leafy branches swaying in the breeze, saw the moon beaming between them, and felt blessedly connected to it all. In my brief drinking history, such moments of spiritual euphoria were common.

"Do you believe in God?" I asked, awaiting his zip and turn.

"Who cares if I believe there's a God?" he replied as we resumed our mission. "Of course there's a fucking God!" He stretched his arms out to his sides and twirled, tripping and nearly falling. "Look at all this. The sky, the trees, the air. There's a God, all right. A mean, fucking practical joker of a

God. An all powerful blind ass yank-your-chain God." His voice rose as if to be sure the Creator got every word.

He then stopped in his tracks, leaned back and screamed at the top of his lungs—no words, just a string of unintelligible vowels, a cry of agony I drunkenly mistook for silliness.

"I have no response to that," I replied.

We purchased our stogies and zig-zagged down Main Street, puffing away. At the edge of town, past the railroad tracks and the beer distributor, Ransom ducked down a thin, gravel trail between the Catholic church and Owen's Dry Cleaners.

We emerged into a hidden clearing I discovered was a cemetery. I squatted and strained to see the nearest scarred headstone, 'Hannah, wife of Lewis Griffith.' I read the epitaph aloud:

Farewell, my husband, you I leave
Though sad and surely you may grieve
This grave contains your humble bride
And your sweet babe lies by my side.

It was dated 1838.

"Man, this place is old," I noted as I stood.

"I found it my first week at Harrison," Ransom explained. "I come here to be with my mother. Crazy, huh? I come to a place 500 miles from where she's buried just to talk to her."

Somehow, I knew not to say anything, nor to ask any of the questions. He turned away, the camaraderie of the evening lost in the depth of his reflection. There were no more Van Morrison debates or spontaneous philosophical discourses. There was only silence and the faint outline of a dead woman's ghost. The wind turned colder and I shivered as we retreated back to campus.

❧

Lawford Hall sat on the entrance edge of the campus, perfectly parallel with Amberson Chapel. When visitors arrived, this was the building where they first stopped. It housed the offices of the president and his assistant, the Alumni Relations staff, Student Affairs Personnel and the *Harrison Herald,* and looked from a distance, and even up close, like a medieval monastery. It also contained the auditorium that, by day, was the drafty, dungeon-house of torturous accounting classes. Soon, it became my own private Radio City Music Hall.

Since orientation, I had seen the signs advertising a freshman talent contest, but only found the courage to enlist the day before. Though I had happily performed for family and friends since childhood, three hundred strangers was a different matter all together.

"I'm old enough to vote now, and fight my country's wars," I sang when my turn finally arrived, a telling tremolo in my voice, my nervous fingers moving awkwardly along the fret board. "And soon I'll be allowed to use the local liquor stores."

I selected a song called *Dear David* I wrote the summer before. It was a musical letter to my deceased younger brother and brought him up to speed on all that was happening in our family. By the time I strummed the final chord my nervousness had been replaced by genuine emotion and I stood, swallowing my throat, as the audience cheered.

I returned my guitar to its case and left the building through the stage doors, flying from my first taste of public approval. I hurried around to the main entrance and sneaked into the auditorium, taking a seat in the last row just in time to catch the end of the final contestant's song. He had a beautiful, silky-smooth voice and sang with conviction about his personal Savior. Ransom sat down beside me.

"Is that true?" he asked when the lights came up. The judges had adjourned to deliberate. "Did your brother really die?"

"Yeah," I said. "When we were kids."

"How?" These were the first personal questions Ransom had asked me. I was unaccustomed to being the object of his focus.

"Meningitis," I replied. "He just didn't wake up one morning."

"How old?"

"Eighteen months. I was three."

The din around us escalated as students stood and milled about the sloped assembly hall floor. I noticed Matt Price listening solemnly to a fellow short-hair. I could only imagine what they were discussing.

"How'd your mother die?" I asked.

"She drowned."

"Drowned," I parroted.

"Drowned," he repeated.

"How old were you?"

"Sixteen. It was four years ago this month."

A hush fell over the room as darkness returned. We stopped our exchange and watched the president of the Student Governing Association take center stage and begin his closing spiel, thanking the judges and all of the brave, talented souls who had "strutted their stuff." I was stunned when he announced that I had taken second prize, and found my way in a daze to the stage where I was handed a check for twenty five dollars.

Ransom shook my hand. "Want to go for a victory drive?"

"Sure. Where are we gonna find a car?"

"I have a car," he stated matter-of-factly.

We found his tan, four-door, 1972 Plymouth Scamp in Siberia, the student parking lot along the northern ridge of the campus.

"I bought it last summer from an old lady who hardly ever drove it," he said, explaining the automobile's excellent condition. "It only has twenty thousand miles on it."

The steering wheel looked like it belonged on a bus and the front seat felt like a big, vinyl coffin. Ransom reached into the back and pulled out two 12 ounce Budweisers.

"Cheers," he said, before taking the first sip.

We drove aimlessly through the maze of back roads. My sense of Pembrook's status as an isolated small town became more acute with each passing cornfield. Houses were definitely the exception, not the rule. At an early stop sign Ransom put the car in park and set his first empty on the floor. Placing his foot atop it, he touched the sides lightly with his index fingers and the can collapsed easily beneath his weight. I chugged the remains of mine and did the same.

"Shove the empties under the seat," he directed.

We continued our drive through the moonlit countryside, drinking our beers and listening to classic rock on an AM radio station. I was thrilled to be creating a life of adventure away from my home and my old friends. I was proud to have attained the acceptance of this person—two years my elder—I had chosen for my surrogate brother. I was slightly buzzed, happy and alive.

At one point, Ransom surprised me by saying, "My mother was a poet. There's a poem of hers in the anthology Exley uses."

"Pretty serious," I commented.

"She was serious all right...the genuine real deal. When I was a kid I remember our house being full of her friends and her sitting in the middle of the room reciting something. It felt like listening to really good old music. She was tapped in, man."

At that moment it was like a third person joined us in the car: Ransom's sadness. The shift was so dramatic a lump formed in my throat—and I'd never even met the woman. I combated the mood swing by offering some autobiographical tidbits of my own.

"My Aunt Nancy was a contestant on *The Price Is Right* last year."

Nothing.

"My dad's the principal of the school we all went to. Wasn't that bad, though. Everybody liked him."

Still nothing.

"I can't believe I got second prize."

Ransom seemed to grow less sullen. Once the last beer can was stashed, he pulled over to relieve himself. I sat alone in the still-running car when I saw the flashing red light approaching from the rear. It was attached to a Pembrook County Police car.

As the single lawman neared us, cool-hand Ransom yelled in a sober sounding voice, "Lost a hubcap."

There was no response. A flashlight beam danced through the Scamp's dull interior before falling on my expressionless face. The absence of anything incriminating seemed to satisfy the officer, who looked as if his testicles had not yet dropped.

"Any luck?" came his good-natured reply.

I was half tempted to yell out to Ransom, "Hey, it's Gomer Pyle," but I thought that might hurt our chances for a clean get-away.

"Nah," came the comfortable reply. "I think I'll have to come back tomorrow. Find it in the daylight."

The young cop offered to help but Ransom put him off, saying, "I'm not even sure this is where it came off. Better just come back tomorrow. Thanks though."

The six beers I'd consumed, along with my talent show triumph and our run-in with the law, convinced me that the night was mine and that romance awaited. Back on campus, I coaxed Ransom into going with me to the tail end of a dance in Kessler Rec.

We stood in the corner, drunken wallflowers, and I scanned the floor for faces I recognized. In my head, I converted the small, square directory pictures to life size and searched for matches. I was really looking for Lynn Cussimano (English Major, Toledo, Ohio), with whom I had actually spoken one day as we left the Religious Philosophy class we shared. She was the current leader in the race to be my soul mate.

I spotted her dancing with a female friend in the middle of the crowded room. When the next slow song began, I made my move. I tapped her on the shoulder, interrupting her conversation, and asked, "Can I have this dance?"

"Why, certainly," she replied, her face beaming with friendliness. About halfway through the song we seemed to instinctively pull each other closer. I closed my eyes and breathed in the smell of her hair. Herbal Essence.

The song ended and Lynn asked, "Can we step outside for a minute?" This was going even better than I'd hoped. Standing in the cool, night air, I gazed into her almond eyes awaiting her cue. After what seemed an eternity she said, "Have you been drinking, Finbar?"

It gets fuzzy after that. She became the missionary and I the unconverted native. I mostly tuned out her speech, which revolved around her God and her values and the dangers of alcohol and the fact that I had held her too closely. It became the sound the TV makes when a station runs a test of the emergency broadcasting system.

Finally, sensing a pause that might have been a conclusion, I said, "I'm sorry, Lynn. I did have a little too much to drink tonight. It won't happen again."

I started smiling then; not the conciliatory, self-deprecating smile I intended, but, instead, a shit-eating, maniacal smile that served to undermine the sincerity of my words. I couldn't help it, though. I was suddenly euphoric.

"You don't look sorry." She turned and strode off in the direction of her dorm.

❧

Back at the dance, Ransom was nowhere to be found. Wanting to tell him about my brush with the moral majority and my strange reaction to it, I left the noisy rec hall and made for our dorm. Before I reached it, though, I saw him in the distance, standing in the center of the East Quadrangle. His arms were outstretched and his face was pointed toward the heavens. Slowly, gracefully, in eerie stillness, his body fell backwards and met the soft earth.

Chapter Two

Monday evening I tapped on Ransom's door. As I waited in the hall, I heard him sit up in bed, then his footsteps crossing the floor. He stood in the doorway wearing a t-shirt and underwear, his eyes barely opened, an emblazoned cigarette butt clamped between his pale lips. I watched, fascinated, as he ingested the precious nicotine.

"Those things'll kill you, you know?" I warned.

"Finbar," he said grumpily, "what do you want?"

"Just wanted to see what you were up to," I replied, ignoring his tone. "Thought maybe you'd want to get some dinner. Where'd you disappear to Saturday?"

"Couldn't bear to see you get your heart broken," he said, squint-smiling as part of his next deep intake.

He grabbed a pair of jeans from the back of his only chair and put them on as I entered his modest hovel. I told him about Lynn Cussimano and my abortive attempt at romance.

"Never make the first move," he dryly proclaimed. "They'll crush you every time."

"I don't know," I replied. "You don't seem to be beating them back with a stick or anything."

The room was better lit than the last time I had seen it. A

naked bulb in the center of the ceiling cast an abundance of indiscriminate light, not that there was much to see. My eyes were drawn to the photographs above his bed. The bigger one, 5″ by 7″, was a black-and-white headshot of a woman who looked to be in her late twenties. Her hair was short and black and she smiled, slightly, like Mona Lisa.

"This your mom?"

"Yeah," he said. "That's the picture they used on the jacket of her first big collection. Rosemary Gardner, queen of the malcontents."

"Who's this?" I asked, pointing to the smaller, more modern-looking photo.

"Maggie Stuard," he replied. "She's a senior."

"She your girlfriend or something?"

"'Or something'. We hung out together a little bit last year."

"What happened?"

"I don't know," he replied. "I just wasn't up for the whole boyfriend-girlfriend thing, I guess."

A cloud of smoke indicated that this chapter of our conversation had concluded.

🍁

Pizza House stood at the corner of Main and Elm. On a slow Monday evening, we had it to ourselves. We ordered a large pepperoni and sat in the center of the dining room, surrounded by yellow and green wallpaper flowers.

Ransom lit up. Dark lines underscored his gray-blue eyes. A thin, disorganized goatee surrounded his mouth. He didn't look at me directly, opting instead to survey the imaginary distance, through the red-lettered window, past the picturesque street outside, his breathing even and slow.

"Ever read *Great Expectations?*" I asked, feeling the need

to re-break the ice. Dr. Mabry had been leading our Lit class through the murky but colorful world of Pip and Joe Gargary.

"Yeah," he replied, "great book. My mom and dad used to read Charles Dickens to me every Saturday night when I was a kid. That was my big weekend entertainment."

"Why'd they name you Ransom? They ever tell you?"

"One of my mom's poems. She had a line about paying off a ransom with barrels filled with heather. She knew from the moment she was pregnant she'd call me that.

"Better than Heather," I joked.

"Seventeen, pepperoni," yelled the man behind the counter in a thick Italian accent. I wondered how Pembrook had landed such an authentic sounding pizza man. The first bite of the salty pie burned my mouth's tender roof. That always seemed to happen.

"My dad wasn't in any condition to talk her out of it at the time," Ransom continued on an uncharacteristic roll. "He used to drink. He's been sober for as long as I can remember, but apparently he used to be a real boozehound. Now he's Mister AA. He goes to meetings all the time, more since my mom died." He gave his dwindling cigarette one last suck, causing its frazzled gray end to turn orange. "My father," he proceeded, "my poor father. He had to fall in love with a crazy woman."

"Your mom was crazy?"

"Oh yeah," he replied without hesitation. "Certifiable. It was like growing up in an asylum, for Christ's sake. One minute she'd be cooking us dinner and the next minute she'd be cutting her hair with a steak knife. She was crazy all right." He smothered the stub of his cigarette in the tin ashtray. "Sometimes I think I'm following in her footsteps."

With these words he closed down, his urge to share disintegrating before my eyes. I waited for a moment but quickly realized that he was through for the evening. I may as well have been sitting alone. I carried on through the remainder of the meal, talking a little, but mostly just eating. Ransom barely touched his food.

Walking back to our dormitory, I contemplated my puzzling, inscrutable friend. His brief disclosures gave some insight into his muted approach to life, but not enough.

❧

"Collect call for anyone from Charles, Prince of Wales. Do you accept the charges?" I heard the operator inquire just after eleven that night.

"I'll accept the charges," Sara replied, giggling.

"Hey, Sar," I said, the first words I had spoken to her since she'd left me three weeks before.

"How's it going, Finbar?" she asked in a sweet voice, excited that I had called for her and not my parents who would have been asleep for an hour at least. I pictured her cherubic face smiling as she sat cross-legged on the purple shag-carpeted floor of her bedroom. Gossip Central.

"Not too bad. I think I'm starting to like it here. What's going on with you?"

"Danielle's been talking behind my back again," she began and proceeded to summarize her life's top stories. "Are you making new friends?"

"Did mom tell you to ask me that?"

My mother often accused me of being too shy, especially in situations that made me uncomfortable. She was right, of course.

"Yeah, I'm making new friends." My mind's eye flashed on Ransom and myself, walking back from town that evening, and then to Matt Price polishing his belt buckle Sunday morning. "I doubt I'll get elected class president or anything, but I'm doing all right. Let mom know, okay?"

"I miss you, Finbar," she said before we hung up. "Thanks for calling."

"I miss you too, Sar," I replied.

❧

— "Christ, does the sun ever stop shining here, Ransom?"

— "Mind if I tag along?"

— "Hey, Ransom, where you headed?"

Each of these questions was on the tip of my tongue at some point the next morning after I spotted Ransom heading toward the bottom of campus. And each one dissolved, unspoken, as 'catching up' became 'following,' which, in turn, became 'spying.' He took the same sidewalk we'd traveled the night before. Instead of turning right and proceeding into town, though, he crossed the street and continued straight. I trailed him by a good fifty feet, just keeping him in my sight.

His trek ended in the Esther Salerno Memorial Park, which I had not known existed until that moment. A trio of smiling mothers stood together, gazing on their mingling children. I hid behind the trunk of an oak and watched as Ransom took a seat at a square stone table. Across from him sat an old man who wore, among other things, a tattered jean jacket and a plaid cap. They greeted each other with familiar nods and turned their attention to the chessboard between them. I observed the innocent scene a few minutes then, embarrassed by my nosiness, slunk away. Back in Jefferson, I heard our hall phone ring as I reached my floor.

"Is Ransom Seaborn there?" came the question from a female voice on the other end.

"No he's not, can I take a message?" I replied politely, a little out of breath.

"Just tell him Maggie called, please."

I wanted to say something then, compare notes, ask her

if she knew about Ransom's illicit chess activity, but all that came out was, "Sure thing."

❧

I couldn't shake the image of Ransom and the old man. Leave it to Ransom—the silent specter of Harrison College, the loner who had no friends, about whom people fabricated dark myths—to hook up with an elderly townsman and become his chess partner. They probably meet there every week, I thought as I entered Underhill on the way to my Religious Philosophy class.

"Hi, Finbar." These words, issuing forth from Lynn Cussimano's beatific face, broke off my pointless rumination.

"Hi, Lynn," I replied, surprise turning to shame in the second it took to remember our run-in the Saturday before. What could I possibly have been thinking, asking her to dance like that?

"Did you start studying for the test yet?" she asked, her moralistic rebuke water under the proverbial bridge. "I hear Dr. Phillips gives pretty rough exams."

"A little," I answered, forcing my eyes up from the floor.

❧

The red numbers of my bedside clock read 2:37. I'd been trying to sleep for more than two hours. Rather than continue my frustrating attempts to decipher Matt's intricate pattern of whistles, snores and moans, I dressed quietly and went outside. The campus was silent, peaceful and still, with just the faint trace of a breeze blowing through: the promise of autumn.

I opened my empty mailbox in Alumni. I studied Underhill's distinctive scent—a combination of chalk dust, felt eras-

ers, old maps and new books. I watched a custodian slosh
soap into small rivers, which he then made smooth and neat
with the heavy swag of his industrial grade cotton mop. I be-
held the towering splendor of Amberson's illuminated stee-
ple.

My roving concluded in Kessler Rec, where I spotted Ransom slumped over a desk in the corner. Moving closer, I saw
he was asleep, his calm face resting on an open brown book.
I had yet to see him do conventional schoolwork but often
caught him scribbling away in what I assumed was a journal
of some sort. Staring down at him, I saw the child he had once
been, and not the brooding introvert I'd come to know. He
looked peaceful and untroubled. The illusion broke when he
jumped awake, startling the hell out of me.

"Finbar," he said. "What are you doing here? What time
is it?"

"Nearly four o'clock," I said softly, still recovering from
the scare. "You must have been having a nightmare."

"What else is there?"

"Better get to bed, man."

"Yeah," he agreed, standing to follow. "Better get to bed."

❧

Wednesday morning I filed into Creative Writing with the
last stragglers as Dr. Exley, perched on the edge of his desk,
collected our papers. Behind great rectangles of glass his eyes
squinted as his lip rode up, his entire face pinched in concentration. He was attempting to make out the words of a female
student in the second row. Once he registered the fact that
she was explaining to him why she had failed to complete
the assignment, his face relaxed, giving way to a half-lidded
expression of bored intolerance. He listened to her excuses

and plea-bargaining with no trace of interest, interrupting her with non-sequiturs and absurd rants.

"The thing is," she explained. "I've been so busy these last couple of days, and—"

"Has anyone ever looked up the word spleenwort?" he asked.

"Dr. Exley, I know there's no—"

"No one?"

"See, I had this paper for Dr. Messer, and I must—"

"Dr. Messer?" he asked, finally responding to her directly. "Dr. Eugene W. Messer III? Have you ever noticed how he puts that damned 'III' at the end of his name? Every damn time. He's sending us a memo on the brand of toilet paper in the Fine Arts Building and he signs it, 'Dr. Eugene W. Messer III.' I'm a third. Dr. Frederick P. Exley III. But I don't find the need of it's cumbersome little tag-on for every salutation and introduction."

By this time, many of us were smiling. Remarkably, the timid instigator of the doctor's humorous attack persisted in her self-defense.

"I think it was for oral interp—"

"Oral interp?" he interrupted again. "Have you ever thought what a provocative title that is? To interpret orally. Just what do you interpret in there? And Dr. Eugene W. Messer III teaching it. Tell me, dear, do you imagine Dr. Eugene W. Messer III would know how to respond to an oral interpretation if it came up and grabbed him in the…"

Presumably, he'd seen enough in her face to delight him, and relented, saying, "Oh, well, now I don't want to sully, to taint, any of our virgin and burgeoning minds. My apologies." He then proceeded with his lesson for the day.

I ate lunch at the deserted end of a table in Block. As I finished my meal, Ransom sat down across from me. I proceeded to recount Dr. Exley's comical interrogation of the unsuspecting Harrisonette. Ransom smiled obligingly.

"Well, I better be hitting the books," I said. "I have that test tomorrow in Religious Philosophy."

He nodded as I stood to leave.

"Did you get the message that Maggie called?" I asked before turning away.

"Yeah," he replied. "Thanks."

❧

I studied in the library until evening, then migrated through the balmy, star-filled night to the Podunk—the crowded, clustered, yellow-lit campus epicenter. It was as busy as I had ever seen it. All of the square and round wooden tables were filled. As I prepared to take my leave, I heard my name being called.

"Finbar, over here," Lynn Cussimano repeated from the middle of the room where she was seated along with three others I recognized from our Religious Philosophy class. "Want to study with us?" she asked, her ever-present smile willing me closer.

"Sure," I replied and took the only available chair.

"Greg, Emily, Jennifer, this is Dan Finbar," Lynn exclaimed as murmured greetings were issued all around. I sensed that these classmates all shared Lynn's close connection with the risen Lord.

"We just got to the Reformation," Emily explained. "What's your take on Luther?"

So began my first true interaction with the student body. And though I had a feeling they might all pray for my poor, lost soul the instant I left their presence, it felt good to be a part of something—even a simple study group. We grilled each other contentedly until the Podunk closed at midnight.

❧

The test went well. College exams would not be the impossible challenge I'd feared. As I left the classroom Thursday afternoon and walked out into the sunshine, victory and relief combined to form exhilaration. I jogged back to the dorm. As I passed Ransom's door, I knocked.

"You there, Ransom?" I yelled, bolder than I'd been before kicking the ass of my first major college examination.

"Door's open."

He sat on the floor with his legs extended and his back leaning against the bed. His open journal rested on his lap and his head was tilted back upon the mattress top, as if he were studying the ceiling.

"You wanna catch some football?" I asked.

After giving the matter serious consideration he said, "Yeah, I'll catch some football with you."

The way he answered made it sound like I could have asked him anything. "You wanna shoot some heroin?" "Yeah, I'll shoot some heroin with you." "You wanna hitchhike to California?" "Sure, I'll hitchhike to California with you."

I went to grab my football and we headed down to the lawn outside our dorm. In the cruel, quiet way men have of assessing each other's athletic skills, I surmised that Ransom was a good athlete. Soon we were running patterns and taking pride in our more challenging catches.

As our energy flagged beneath the deadening afternoon sky, a co-ed traversing the distant sidewalk yelled, "Hey, Ransom!" He lifted his right arm in reply and turned away.

"Is that Maggie?" I asked as we strolled back into Jefferson.

"Yes," he answered, sadly, I thought.

❧

Matt and I watched TV and had pizza delivered to our room that night.

"I saw you catching football with Ransom Seaborn today," he said at commercial. "How'd you manage to pierce the veil?"

I pulled a Ransom and remained silent.

"What's he like?" he asked, not buying my routine.

"I don't know," I replied. "Why don't you ask him yourself?"

"Don't be an asshole. What's he like?"

Just as Matt's casual wear seemed forced, so, too, did his cursing. No matter how often he swore, it always sounded like the first time.

"What's it to you?" I asked.

"I'm just curious. Is he as strange as he seems?"

"He's no stranger than you," I replied, an unexpected edge surfacing in my voice. "He's just quiet, Matt. Cut him some slack."

"Someone told me he's a drug addict," he added, ignoring me. "Is he a drug addict?"

"No, Matt, he's not a drug addict. And he didn't kill anybody in high school, and he's not in the witness relocation program," I snapped. "Give the guy a break. He's just quiet."

"I was just asking," he responded. "No need to get pissy."

Our verbal sparring concluded when we heard an ominous, soft knocking on our door. Visitors were not exactly common at room 223 and we looked at each other, puzzled. Ransom stood in the hallway. Dressed in his standard black boots, black jeans, and black t-shirt, he looked like a young, strung out Johnny Cash. His unexpected appearance seemed to send a shiver through Matt, who took a step back and opened his mouth, as if the devil himself had come calling.

"Here's that CD I borrowed," he said, stepping into the room and extending his hand. "Thanks."

"What'd you think?" I asked, accepting the disc—The Silos, *Cuba.*

"Perfect," he replied, tossing an 'I just might have killed somebody in high school and I just might kill you too' look at Matt, who shrank back from him. "Later."

❦

A cool breeze awakened me an hour early on Friday morning. I sat on the edge of my bed considering the day ahead. Three classes in the morning and then the long weekend begins, I thought, ignoring the existence of Saturday morning Accounting. I felt good. After hitting the bathroom, I pulled on my trustiest pair of Levis and a Neil Young concert t-shirt I'd borrowed permanently from my brother, and headed off to MAP to get some breakfast.

I sat alone in the cafeteria and shoveled cereal from bowl to mouth as I continued *Great Expectations.* Pip had just fallen victim to Miss Havisham's evil games and to Estelle's unattainable beauty. The entire female world was Estelle to me, beautiful and unattainable. I related.

The chapel service for the morning featured a famous theologian who would be lecturing on campus that night. The place was jammed. I braced myself for another dose of thinly veiled condescension but was captivated by the man's passion and humor. He made a common sense plea to all Christians to live like Christ, and seemed to fly in the face of the loftier, more judgmental 'Religious' to whom I had become accustomed. I made a mental note of the time he'd be speaking that evening and moved with the herd back into the sunlight.

❧

Dr. Mabry shared my deep sympathy with the fledgling Pip. She opened her class by saying, "Women can be cruel and heartless. Pip never had a chance."

"Amen, sister!" I shouted in my head.

Dr. Rider got sidetracked from the Russian Revolution to a used car dealership in town and never made it back. I barely heard a word he said.

In Creative Writing, the blinds were drawn. Dr. Exley explained, "I teach a film class in this very room the period before this." Dramatic pause. "Today we watched a wonderful piece by Buster Keaton." Dramatic pause. "I enjoyed it so thoroughly, I want to see it again. Any objections?"

"None here," I chimed, again only to myself.

❧

Joining the right lane of the two-way sidewalk traffic, I went to Alumni to check my mail. I saw Ransom approaching from the opposite direction, slightly hunched, smoking and walking with a single-minded intensity. He didn't see me, though, and I had no reason to track him down.

I was pleasantly surprised to find a letter in my mailbox from Steve Clark. It began: "This week has definitely been a strange one since the delta of the Mississippi moved into my apartment." He went on to describe the latest woman of his dreams (he was another hopeless Estelle worshipper) and wondered if I had recovered from my infatuation with Lisa Starzel, the girl I had longed for the summer before.

"I'm coming home the last weekend in October, Fin. Let's

all do something." By 'all,' he meant the small band of misfits we'd assembled over the past seven years: Ronny Boyle, the Sebastian twins, Mike Imuso. I smiled, picturing our drunken reunion.

❧

I couldn't stomach the idea of another meal alone in the school cafeteria and decided to grab a bite at The Pembrook Diner instead. I dropped my books in my room, with the exception of *Great Expectations,* and made the half-mile walk.

By the time I pushed open the squeaky screen door, it was 1:30. The room stretched out before me in a long, narrow rectangle. I took the vinyl-upholstered window booth second from the entrance. Two old men smoked and talked at the table to my right. They scrutinized a picture, apparently of a newborn baby, on the cover of the local newspaper.

"That's a sincerian," the one with his back to me announced in a disproportionately loud voice. "No wrinkles."

"A Syrian?" the other one replied, not quite so loud, but close. He winked at me, having fun at his friend's expense.

"No, a sincerian. I once saw a baby three hours old, looked a month old, mother had a C-section, no wrinkles." He sat back in his chair, then added, "It's cause it don't come out the normal way."

"But what do the Syrians have to do with it?" his counterpart asked, chuckling now.

I smiled.

A thick, severe-looking waitress barreled through the two-way kitchen doors, carrying slices of pumpkin pie on small plates. She slapped the deserts down before the men.

"That's a cesarean all right," she spat, stressing the 'cesarean' so they'd be sure and catch the proper pronunciation. The name on her blouse said 'Stella,' and I wondered if it was short for Estelle. She gave new meaning to the word 'gruff' and took my order without quite acknowledging my presence, as though if she didn't actually see me, it wouldn't qualify as work. As she hurried away, I buried my head in my book and looked up only when she returned, ten minutes later, to hoist a burger and fries onto my table.

"Will there be anything else?" she asked, finally looking at me.

"No," I said meekly.

"Have a nice day, hon." She handed me the bill.

🍁

Sweat formed on my forehead as I walked down Main Street. It was eighty degrees, at least. CJ's Music Mine was tucked between the Meats-n-More Deli and the Ithen Printing Shop, just as Matt had promised. Its walls were covered with outdated posters and the shelves were practically empty. In keeping with the rules of providence, however, their meager stock included one Van Morrison, the very one I'd been meaning to acquire, *Veedon Fleece.* Happily, I handed my money to the pimply-faced cashier in exchange for the brown paper bag that held the coveted music.

I enjoyed the slow journey back to campus, stopping frequently to look at anything that caught my eye: an outdoor grade school gym class; an ancient husband and wife shuffling into the Food Lion; a blue jay landing on a telephone wire. It was a beautiful afternoon.

When I got back to Jefferson, I headed straight for Ransom's room; anxious to see if he'd ever heard *Veedon Fleece,* and wondering if he'd be interested in a little Friday afternoon happy hour. I didn't even knock.

As my hand turned the doorknob, I heard a deafening explosion. The timing was such I almost thought that I had caused it. I jumped backwards, letting myself believe for a moment that it had come from just outside, just below Ransom's window, and not from the room within. When I opened the door, my deepest fears were confirmed and my life was changed forever.

Ransom Seaborn had killed himself.

❦

Five days until Christmas; I failed to mention that before. The Main Street lampposts are draped in garland and lights. I walked through town at 4 am conducting my landmark inventory. CJ's, Pizza House, the diner—they're all still there, only slightly the worse for wear. I observed it all silently, my thoughts a low, whirring, wordless drone.

Lazy-eyed Lou is short, bald and stocky. He moves forward and backward on the balls of his feet when he talks, and keeps his hands in his pockets. He is the Cloverleaf's only employee. He stops me on my way back from each coffee run—no matter the time—to offer some question, insight, or detail of his life.

This is what I've learned so far: His wife left him years ago, shortly after they were married. He worked for the Port Authority in Pittsburgh for twenty-five years and receives monthly pension checks. (I could tell you the exact amount, but that wouldn't be right.) He has no children or siblings and enjoys his status as a completely unencumbered human being. He has an almost motherly concern for my well being and is a fundamentally kind, simple man. He is Italian.

"There's a coffee maker in the office," he said to me this morning, nodding at my giant CoGos cup. "You can take it to your room if you want. I got coffee." I was, after all, the motel's only guest. "What are you doing in there?" he asked.

"Writing my memoirs," I answered dryly, not surprised by his blunt question.

"I been thinkin' about doin' that myself," he said thoughtfully. He noticed my wedding ring then. "Married?" he asked, other questions implied but unspoken. He was obviously eager for the scales of disclosure to balance.

"Yes," I said, and then said nothing more.

I wanted to tell Lou the story of my ninth Christmas. I'm not sure why. It just popped into my head—because of the holidays, I guess. Lou seems like the kind of guy who wouldn't mind an irrelevant story.

My family attended Christmas Eve mass that year, then gathered in the living room to exchange our grab bag gifts. Ann, the oldest, presented first. Before she could complete her turn we heard a loud engine motoring up our dead end street, and ran to the window. Through heavy snowflakes we saw a car slide to a halt and a lone man emerge. He sprinted down into the white-blanket field beyond the last well-lit home and disappeared as two whining police cars tore up the road. The first one braked too late and crashed with a loud thud into the fugitive's parked vehicle. Four officers emerged, briefly surveyed the damage, and then followed their quarry's tracks into the distance.

The image is frozen in my memory: the street lit by the potent combination of moon and snow; the two sirens spinning red and blue; the four men holding guns, preparing for dangerous pursuit; the winter night's violated silence. A surge of electricity ran through Vance Street as people halted their Holiday traditions to stare, side by side, at the Christmas adventure that had been delivered to their doorsteps. Phone calls were made, notes compared. Pieces of the puzzle began to appear. The man had robbed Saint Augustine's rectory. He'd pointed a gun at Father Worthman and commanded him to hand over the collection money. He was an escaped convict. He was spotted lurking in the back of the church during the very mass we had attended.

After he was apprehended and the vehicles cleared from the street, the excitement lingered. Our senses had been heightened, our feeling *of togetherness sweetened. That's what I remember most from that night. As we finished our gift exchange, we knew we were a family and took comfort in the knowledge.*

My ninth Christmas…

Where were we? Oh yes, the big moment: Ransom's suicide. Did I surprise you there? I had hoped to convey some of the shock I felt. I was just beginning to get my bearings, finally starting to feel like I belonged. One deafening explosion sent me tumbling back to zero.

Chapter Three

The sunny days ended the Monday after Ransom died. A cold rain fell on the bulk of the student body as we shuffled into Amberson Chapel, a feeling of violation permeating the collective psyche. I was numb. I stood beside Matt as, from the wooden pulpit, Dr. Phillips and Reverend Jones spouted platitudes. Their thin lips moved, but I heard nothing save the vague, seductive sounds of Christian comfort.

It had been that way Saturday as well. They came to our room and tried to 'get through to me,' their flushed faces, pained and sympathetic; their voices a meaningless, babbling brook. Matt later told me the only thing I needed to have heard: They had made an appointment for me to meet with a local psychiatrist to "ensure that I dealt with the trauma of my discovery."

Monday morning they tried again to bring sense to the "terrible tragedy." I stared blankly at the circular lights dangling from the slanted ceiling. I counted the darkened lines on the back of the pew in front of mine. I read the words on the nearest stained glass window. I listened to my own breathing and the sound of the raindrops on the roof. A silly poem my mother used to recite floated through my head: *Moses supposes his toeses…*

As we filed out of our seats, I felt a gentle tug on my jacket sleeve. "Are you Dan Finbar?" the woman asked, knowing the answer, not waiting to hear it. "Could we talk a minute?"

We flowed with the pedestrian traffic stream up to Alumni Hall and sat at a circular table in a corner of the Podunk. Life went on around us. People chattered, opened mail, ate bagels, oblivious to all that had shattered.

In those moments I saw her up close for the first time: long, brown hair pulled back in a pony tail, piercing blue eyes that beamed out above chapped lips and slanted jaw bones. Her demeanor was sad and tired: she looked like a grieving china doll.

"I'm Maggie," she said. "I was a friend of Ransom's."

"Finbar," I replied. My voice sounded raspy, strange to my ears. "How are you doing?"

"I've been better, Finbar," she understated. "How about you?"

There was nothing but sympathy in Maggie's soft voice. She, like everyone else on campus, knew that I had found him just seconds after the shot was fired. Wherever I walked, I felt their eyes watching me.

"I'm not sure."

Muffled names were called over the PA, orders ready. Gray light fell through the massive square windows.

"Do you know if they found his journal?" she asked

"I don't think so," I replied. "I went to his room Saturday afternoon to see if it was there but I couldn't find it."

I had gone through Ransom's desk and dresser drawers, amazed by the meagerness of his possessions: two pairs of jeans, half a dozen shirts, socks, underwear, three virgin-looking text books and a worn copy of *The Sun Also Rises*. No journal. No mattress on the bed frame or stains on the cold floor.

"Do you think his dad has it?"

"No. He got there just as I was leaving." I pictured Mr. Seaborn as he had looked that day, a waste of a man, eyes vacant and hand trembling as it lifted a cigarette to his mouth. I sought Ransom in that gesture but couldn't find him. Mr. Seaborn looked as if he were about to say something, but didn't. I brushed his arm as I passed him in the doorway.

"God, Finbar, why did he do this?" Maggie asked.

"I don't know. I really didn't see it coming." I couldn't seem to find the volume knob for my voice.

"What was he thinking? Why couldn't he just talk to someone?" She looked like a child who was confounded by a puzzle piece that wouldn't fit, a friend who wouldn't play properly. "Why didn't I do anything to help him?"

"What could you have done?" I asked.

I knew what I could have done. I could have gotten to his room thirty seconds earlier, opened his door thirty seconds before I did, seen the glaring, fucking neon signs.

"I don't know," she replied. "Forced him out of himself or something. I don't know."

Silence again. I checked a wall clock and realized I was missing my Lit class. I didn't care.

"How did you ever get to know him?" I said finally. "He wasn't exactly the friendliest guy in the world."

She smiled as the conversation shifted, the painful present replaced by the past—where Ransom still lived.

"We took a poetry class together first semester last year," she began. "I noticed him talking with Dr. Exley sometimes, but he never talked during class. Then one day Exley asked if anyone knew an entire poem by heart. Ransom raised his hand and recited something his mother had written.

"After class, I followed him to Kessler Rec. I saw him sitting in the corner writing in his journal. I'm almost embarrassed remembering all this, Finbar. I swear I don't usually stalk people. He just intrigued me. I went up and told him how much I loved his poem and asked him what it was. He said it was called *Recovery,* and that his mom wrote it after he was born. He said she was a poet."

"Did he tell you that she died?" I asked.

"Yeah. He told me all kinds of things. He talked about his mom and her accident. He described life in New Hampshire. Said how pretty it was. He talked about his dad. We wound up sitting down by Deer Creek until after it was dark. I couldn't take my eyes off him that day," she said, blushing pale pink. "I don't know what it was. He was so intense and…direct." She spoke slowly, choosing her words carefully. "There was nothing fake about him. And his eyes were so sad. I've never been so affected by a person I just met.

"I felt we had a lot in common, maybe because I lost my mom too, to cancer when I was in High School. Of course, he pretty much became mister invisible again after that day.

"The night before I went home last semester he came to my room drunk. I hadn't seen him since before finals. Something about him was different. He was more restless than usual. He hardly said a word, but I could tell that he was feeling so much." She paused, perhaps remembering that she was talking aloud—to a person she didn't exactly know, then added, "He stayed over that night." The words just hung there. "And he seemed different…in a good way.

"I wrote him a couple of letters over the summer but never heard back. When I saw him on campus this year, he acted like nothing ever happened. Maybe he didn't even remember it. We talked a few times, but not really. I don't think he wanted to be reminded that he'd actually opened up to somebody."

"He kept your picture up," I told her. "Right by his mom's."

"Where the hell is that journal?" she asked, ignoring my consolation. "That was the only thing he cared about. If we could only find his journal, maybe we'd understand a little better."

We sat for a while, absorbed in our thoughts.

"I better get to class," I said finally, standing to leave.

"Thanks for listening, Finbar. Sorry if I rambled."

"No need to be sorry," I replied.

❧

Dr. Exley began his class that day by reading a sad poem Ransom's mom had written.

"I have a hunch Ransom shared his mother's poetic vision," he said afterward. "Genetics are a hell of a thing."

❧

"Your dad called, Fin," Matt said when I got back to the room. "Twice."

My parents were concerned about me, and had telephoned often since hearing of my unfortunate intrusion on Ransom's suicide scene. I dreaded our conversations. I didn't want them to worry, but felt unequal to the task of communicating with them, or with anyone.

"How you doin', Dan?" my father asked ten minutes later, once I'd finally worked up the energy to talk.

"I think I'm all right."

"Your mother and I want to drive up on Friday, get you away from there for the weekend."

On my dad's mood palette, cheerful and concerned were nearly identical.

"My last class ends at 12:30," I replied, still digesting the idea of this impromptu homecoming. Somehow, the thought of being in the safe, familiar confines of my parents' house did not quite jibe with my current state of mind.

"We'll be outside your building a little after that, okay?" He took my silence as consent and continued, "Have you met with the psychiatrist yet?"

Another conversation I dreaded. "No, that's on Thursday."

Suddenly, I was wiped out. It was all I could do to keep my eyes open.

"At some point, you're going to have to talk about what you saw, Dan," he said kindly. "I know it's hard to come to grips with, but you're going to have to."

"I know," I answered mechanically, without thinking. I could have fallen to sleep standing up. "I gotta go, Dad."

"We love you, Dan."

Click.

※

Thursday afternoon I stood outside Jefferson awaiting a ride from Eugene Messer, my faculty advisor. He'd been assigned the task of driving me to my psychiatric evaluation— or whatever it was—in the neighboring town of Angora. We listened to classical music and did not speak on the short drive up Route 79.

"If I give the boy some space," I imagined him thinking, "maybe he'll unburden himself." Everyone, it seemed, was intent on getting me to open up.

Dropping me off he said, "I'll see you in an hour, Dan. Hope all goes well in there."

The office looked and felt like a living room. We sat on worn leather recliners as if awaiting our favorite prime-time programming. Thick medical journals and random works of fiction lined the shelves and covered the desk and window-sills.

Dr. Sussman appeared to be in his late forties. His bulldog

face was partially covered by a gray-peppered black beard and mustache. Brown eyes peered out, warm and concerned, over wire-rimmed bifocals. His voice was a smooth baritone, an afternoon DJ on a soft jazz station.

"Hello, Daniel," he began. "You can call me Jake, by the way." He was going with the informal approach. "Would you prefer if I called you Dan?"

"That'd be fine," I replied, not wanting to go into the whole Finbar thing.

"First of all, I'm sorry for the loss of your friend, and for what you must be going through. A shock like that can be devastating, I know." He sounded sincere. That is to say, he sounded like a human being, not just a psychiatrist. When I didn't respond, he continued, "And I realize this must be hard for you, Dan, just coming here and sitting down with a total stranger. But there's no pressure. We'll only talk about the things you want to talk about. We won't force anything." He looked at me in earnest to determine if the message had been received. "That being said, what can you tell me about last Friday?"

As it turned out, a great deal. I seized the chance to exercise my vocal chords and delivered a lengthy description of classes that morning, lunch in the diner, my visit to the music store and the beautiful walk back to campus. When I got to the part about Ransom, though, I stopped cold, unable to summon the images.

"It's completely natural," he explained, "for our minds to block out or repress painful or disturbing memories. It would be completely understandable if you weren't able to remember what happened next, Dan."

This guy was good. He'd hit the nail on the head. I could see myself walking down the hall, carrying the brown paper bag and turning Ransom's doorknob. I could even hear the sound of the explosion. Then my memory cut to some time later—minutes, hours? When I sat in my room, surrounded by police officers and paramedics, unable to speak, in a state of shock. I didn't explain any of this to the good doctor, of course. I just sat squirming in my seat.

"How well did you know him?" he asked, sensing my inability to go on and wanting me to keep talking. Of course, he didn't realize what a difficult question that was.

But, again, I gushed, describing, in surprising detail, almost every single moment I had spent with Ransom, from the day I spotted him writing in the library, to the afternoon we spent catching football. I told him everything that came into my head. I couldn't stop. Before I knew it, our hour had ended.

"I'd like to see you again, Dan. Do you think we could meet again this same time next week?"

"Sounds good," I replied as I stood to go.

If Messer had expected me to unravel for him on the way back to campus, he was sorely disappointed. My brief period of reckless revelation had come to an end, and I had recommitted myself to a vow of silence. I never saw Dr. Sussman again.

🍁

Late that night I sat in darkness at my desk, the cord from my headphones stretched taut between my ears and the stereo jack. *Veedon Fleece* entered into my muddled consciousness, clearing it out temporarily. I gazed through the window, and the singer's reedy, eerily expressive voice transformed the familiar landscape into rolling green hills of Irish countryside. Separated from my own existence, I fell asleep with my head resting in the crook of my folded arms.

🍁

Friday morning I checked my mailbox for the first time in a week. Among the junk mail was a notice issued by Richard Jones, Director of Public Relations, on the day of Ransom's death. It read:

Accident Report for Campus Community
A student notified Dean of Men Warren Thurber at 4:43 p.m. today that Ransom Seaborn, a junior, communication-arts major had died in Jefferson dormitory at Harrison College of a self-inflicted gunshot wound.
The shot was heard at approximately 4:35 and a fellow student discovered the body shortly thereafter.
According to the rules and regulations published for all students: "Possession and/or use of firearms or other dangerous weapons on College property is prohibited."

6:15 p.m.
Monday regular Chapel period will be a time of prayer instead of the scheduled program.

My parents had taken off work that Friday to come rescue me. I threw my duffel bag into the back seat and took my place beside it. We stopped at the McDonald's drive-thru, then began the ninety-minute drive home. Thankfully, there were no Ransom inquiries. That would come later.

"John got an offer from PJAX," my father announced.

John was my older brother. After graduating college, he took the trucking industry by storm. He seemed to switch companies every few months, always getting better offers.

"I thought he just started with Carolina."

And so we ignored the elephant in the Bonneville. They danced around my sore spot and spared me their scrutiny. Most of the drive was made in comfortable silence.

Sara stood bouncing a basketball in the driveway when we pulled up to the house.

"Finbar," she yelled, a little too enthusiastically, I thought.

"How you doin', Sar?" I asked, hungry for the trivial conversation she gladly provided, filling me in on the details of her week as we shot basketball on our dead-end street. After a game of H-O-R-S-E, we went inside to order pizza, a Friday evening Finbar ritual.

That night we popped popcorn and hunkered down in the living room. Sara lay on the floor. My parents occupied their traditional seats at the head of the room and I sat alone on our threadbare couch. All eyes were glued to the classic Hitchcock film, *Notorious.* All, that is, except for my father's, whose snoring soon blended with the film's dramatic score.

I turned in early, around eleven. My bed felt strange yet familiar: a song I once loved but had not thought of in a long, long time. Drifting off, I remembered the years John and I shared this room, timing the switch from overhead to bedside light ("one, two three…,") talking about daydreams and football games. I had spent more hours in this room than in any other, but now it seemed foreign. Everything seemed foreign. I slept dreamlessly until late the next morning.

❧

All afternoon I studied in the basement, the only refuge from my parents' self-conscious kindness. By nightfall, I desperately needed to get out of the house. I hadn't called anyone to let them know I was coming home and was only able to track down Jay Mosely, who lived in a neighboring plan. I had known Jay since elementary school but had only become friends with him over the past couple of years. Due to our proximity, we had often found ourselves on the same bus rides to and from high school. We'd also played CYO basketball together. Occasionally, we'd passed weekend nights as we planned to pass this one: drinking in the woods behind Saint Augustine's.

Jay had already begun a battle with hair loss. The exposed front of his pate glistened in the moonlight, signaling me like a lighthouse beam through the falling darkness. His older brother had just dropped him off after purchasing a fifth of Southern Comfort for Jay. I don't think he knew that it would only be the two of us.

We found the path opposite the gymnasium doors that led us to our traditional drinking spot, a clearing thirty feet down, which still contained the empty case of Rolling Rock we'd left on our previous visit. We sat on a log and Jay unsealed the bottle.

"So, how's it going at Harrison?" he asked.

He attended a local branch of Penn State and lived at home with his dad and sister. Life away at college intrigued and tantalized him.

"Not too bad. It's not as hard as I thought it might be."

"Is it as strict as they say it is?" If you didn't answer Jay immediately, he would reiterate, clarifying his questions for you, almost apologizing for his curiosity. "You know, everyone says how strict it is there."

In his own way, he was a brilliant conversationalist. He did not abide silence between friends. I told him about the chapel services and the Saturday morning classes.

"In the college handbook, it says that when you're in a girl's room you have to keep the door open six inches and have one foot on the floor at all times." I failed to mention that the women's quarters were off limits all but one night a week.

"Are you shitting me?" he asked, disbelief in his voice.

"And you're not supposed to walk on the grass," I added.

"It's not that bad, though. I'm not sure if they really enforce that stuff."

I took my second swig and winced as the liquor burned down my throat, the evening chill steadily decreasing. Jay proceeded to ponder his own academic situation.

"I don't know, Fin, I just can't get into it," he complained. "I don't think I'm cut out for higher education. I might quit and paint houses with my brother."

"Maybe you should play pro basketball," I suggested.

He had such bad knees that he couldn't have run up the hill if his life depended on it. He laughed.

"I heard about that kid who shot himself," he said, apropos of nothing. I didn't know if that meant he'd heard that I was friends with "that kid who shot himself" and had discovered his dead body, or just that it had happened. Either way, I didn't take the bait.

"Yeah, it was a drag," I replied, the understatement of the year.

As our inhibitions softened, the conversation turned more intimate, at least Jay's end of it. Soon he was being brutally honest about the way his alcoholic mother had emotionally abused his brother, sister and him in the years before she died. And of course, as was always the case when Jay drank, he talked about his true love Patty Kernick, who had broken his heart the winter before.

"Do you think I should call her, Fin? Do you think I should give her a call?"

By the end of the night, an empty bottle sat between us. We stood to leave, leaning on each other for support, and staggered up out of the woods.

In the well-lit school yard I became convinced that I could fly. Taking a running start, I dove headfirst from a foot-high curb. My face, specifically my nose, landed on the pavement before the rest of my body. Jay laughed maniacally as the blood poured through my scraped skin. I lifted my shirt to the open wound and lurched home.

Standing in my parent's kitchen, I screamed at the top of my lungs, "Saul lost his sight on the road to Damascus," over and over.

❧

All good parents give their kids at least two Get Out of Jail Free cards. I received my first the following morning. I stood before my father expecting a reprimand or at least a lecture, but all he said was, "How you feelin', Fin?"

"Not so great."

My visits to the bathroom to vomit had made it into the double digits. Other than the dark red gash across the bridge of my nose, my face was devoid of color. Though spared a lecture, my dad did take it upon himself to share a story.

"In college I roomed my freshman year with a big Texan, Lloyd Becker. He was a real character. One night he surprised me by pulling out a bottle of whiskey."

The sound of the word was almost enough to make me retch.

"I'd had plenty of beer before then, but it was the first time I drank whiskey. Lloyd would take a swig, then hand it to me, and I would take a swig."

Again, I had to consciously hold down the watery sediment in the back of my throat. I wondered if this was a subtle form of torture. Maybe he wasn't being so understanding after all.

"We sat there talking like nothing and before I knew it, we'd killed the bottle. We stood up and Lloyd stepped forward, no problem. I stepped forward and fell flat on my face." He chuckled at his own reminiscence. "It was eleven at night when we finished that bottle, and my room didn't stop spinning until six the next night, nineteen hours later. I haven't tasted whiskey since."

❦

My losing bout with whiskey, though painful and somewhat humiliating, had the good result of keeping my parents from pursuing the Ransom issue. They seemed to sense my physical discomfort and we made the drive back to Pembrook in peace. My mother hugged me, my dad slipped me two twenty-dollar bills, and they left, no questions asked. I followed their departure with my eyes and couldn't help thinking how much had changed since the last time I'd watched them drive away.

❦

"What the hell happened to you?" were Matt's first words upon seeing my disfigured face.

"I got run over by a bulldozer," I replied, flopping down immediately on my unmade bed.

"No, seriously, what happened to you?"

For all his stiffness there was concern in his voice, and I had to accept the fact that this strange guy, who ironed his jeans and with whom I shared close living quarters, was becoming my friend. I gave him a brief synopsis of my ill-fated drinking escapade and could see the level of his sympathy lowering with each word.

"What the hell were you thinking?"

A fair question to which I had no response. He proceeded to inform me of the sibling rivalry that had existed between Isaac Kessler, the first president of Harrison, and his younger brother, Weir. "While Isaac ran the school, Weir earned a fortune in the steel industry in Pittsburgh and donated most of it to Harrison, trying to show up his older brother."

"That's very interesting Matt," I replied, closing my eyes. Moments later, I was sound asleep.

That night I dreamed: The blinds were drawn and taped to the windowpane. Music played softly. His shoulders leaned back against the blood-splattered wall. Blood-stained sheets of yellow hand-written paper were strewn about the bed and floor and on his lap. His chin rested on his still chest, lips closed around the barrel of a .357 Colt revolver. The gun clattered to the floor. His eyes rolled up to stare at me. His lips pulled back, revealing shattered teeth and he began to speak. Softly at first, like a mumbled prayer:

"I will leave this for Finbar,
Then walk to my cell
I will turn on the music
And wish myself well
Swallow my fortune
The barrel, the hole
Run for the river
That carries my soul."

I clapped my hands over my ears and woke up screaming.

Chapter Four

Phil Fercheck's nostrils flared in the center of his round face. This was their natural state. With his desperate, attentive eyes and pinkish complexion he looked like a pig in a spin-cycle washing machine. He stared out helplessly on the mysterious Laundromat world, doomed to observe. Phil was Matt's best friend—his only friend at Harrison other than me. He had driven us to the Sportsman's Club for the Nu Lamb party that night, four weeks and one day after Ransom died.

We had come there, braving the social mainstream, as a result of Matt's concern over my mental and emotional well being. He, more than anyone, witnessed first hand my dovetail into despondency. He had seen me sidestep further visits with Dr. Sussman through a series of well-executed lies, and had awakened to my screams on those rare occasions when I slept deeply enough to dream.

"Come on, Finbar. It'll be fun," he had pleaded. "You need to get out and socialize."

He sounded like my mother.

Two Nu Lambs, dressed in blue and gold jackets, greeted us at the door. Phil continued his discourse on The Eagles as we paid our two bucks and received thick blue 'X's on the tops of our hands.

"They rock," he said for the third time, saliva forming on the edges of his mouth. "I mean they really rock. People don't think that about them, but it's totally true."

We walked down the stairs into an open room filled with college students. The floors were already sticky with spilled beer. Those far enough along in their drinking danced to the up-tempo music blasting through the stereo speakers.

"Have you ever listened to *The Eagles Live?*" Phil screamed as we waited our turn at the keg. His voice had a frequency that bisected my eardrum.

I shook my head and held my cup to be filled by another blue and gold coated brother, who smiled as if to say, "Mother's milk."

"You gotta listen to it," Phil implored, a true zealot. "I'll stop by your room tomorrow and play you some stuff. It totally rocks."

I mumbled something he couldn't possibly have heard and drifted away to lean against the nearest wall, sipping frequently from my plastic cup. By the time I'd gotten my fifth refill, I was happy to be there and content to stand alone, watching the activity around me.

The energy in the room turned more manic with each passing moment. Dancers screamed obscene phrases in unison at key moments of songs. A team of sorority sisters formed a human pyramid, which immediately crashed to the ground, its members laughing uncontrollably.

I noticed Maggie across the room, talking with a handsome fraternity brother. The hair that had been pulled back in a ponytail at our first meeting now flowed freely, thick and naturally curly, down to the small of her back. Otherwise, she looked the same: pale, tired, sad. I checked for telltale signs of coupledom, but saw none.

My buzzed speculation was interrupted by two careening bodies crashing against the wall a foot away from me. It turned out to be an exercise in male bonding. They were practicing an end around or something, an offensive lineman and his prized running back.

Seeing me staring, the bigger of the two, the lineman, said, "You got a problem?"

He wore the color of a different fraternity, crimson. His mood had turned hostile. I didn't say a word.

"Aren't you the kid who found that dude who blew his head off?" He was thrilled with his deduction and looked to his friend, the running back, for confirmation or at least an audience. When I didn't respond, he returned to his first query, embellishing it slightly, "You got a fucking problem?"

Those close enough to hear him over the music stopped their conversations and gave us their full attention. The stage was set for something dramatic to happen. I had never been a fighting man. Thin, quiet, not especially brave or proud, I always walked away. But at that moment, I'd had enough. His dumb meanness and utter lack of sensitivity sent me over the edge. I reached down into that vast reserve of human spirit we possess under duress and punched him in the face with all my might. He fell like a red bag of bricks to the ground as the crowd gasped and murmured around us.

Before the stunned running back could come to his lineman's defense, the beer keg guardian came to mine. As the Nu Lamb closest to the skirmish, he took it upon himself to act as peacemaker, and escorted me from the still-manic scene. I wondered if he was kicking me out, or planning on beating me up himself once we got outside.

My questions were answered the instant the cool air slapped against my face and he said, "Christ you nailed him good," and broke into laughter. "What an asshole!"

I smiled for the first time in a month. A joint materialized in his right hand. He stuck it in his mouth and fired up, sucking in hard. "My name's Dale Fenner," he said, wincing from the smoke, not letting any escape his pursed lips. He passed it over.

"Finbar," I replied, doing as he did, trying not to reveal my status as a rookie dope smoker.

He smiled kindly when I choked on the harsh intake. Though I had no frame of reference, it didn't seem like very good stuff.

"Finbar," he repeated. "Are you some kind of a leprechaun, then?" he asked in a pitiful Irish brogue.

"No, I'm a freshman," I replied, free-associating, causing him to chuckle.

"Well, Finbar," he said, "I'd steer clear of the Okies for a little while. They don't take kindly to one of their own being humiliated in public. In private, it's another matter all together."

We each took one more hit. He wet his fingers and pinched out the lit end of the homemade cigarette. "Catch you later," he said and returned to the party.

Standing alone in the quiet of the night, I stared out at the black hills rolling off into the vast unknown, the great, unfathomable universe. "Is there anything smaller than a speck?" I asked the figureless trees. Their dying leaves rustled in reply. Maggie approached from behind and joined me on the invisible precipice.

"Hi, Finbar," she said. "You all right?"

"I am until that guy sees me again."

I wondered if my words came out slurred. I wondered what she thought of me. I wondered if my head had suddenly quadrupled in size. I wondered if the pot we'd smoked had been very good stuff after all.

"What an asshole," she said. A consensus.

"How have you been?" I asked, putting all of my energy into speaking slowly and clearly.

"I've been better," she confided, glancing up at me, then down, gently drawing on the ground with her right foot. "I still think about him a lot, Finbar."

With the hand closest to me, she brushed her hair back, uncovering her ear. Her face and neck looked silver in the moonlight. Everything looked silver. Party noise persisted in the background. I detected a vague cadence to the mild cacophony. Was I supposed to say something? I couldn't remember which one of us had spoken last.

"I almost called you," she continued, easing my uncertainty, "to apologize for going on like I did in the Podunk that day. You were going through enough without having to hear me ramble on."

Ramble on. Ramble on. What a funny-sounding phrase.

"I think about him, too, Maggie," I exhaled, unaware that I was responding to something she had said minutes ago and sensing, all of a sudden, a powerful dryness in my mouth. Starting with the upper left corner, I began counting my teeth with my tongue.

"I still can't believe he's gone, Finbar. I hardly ever saw him anyway, so I keep expecting to run into him on my way to dinner or something." After an eternity of silence she continued. "The guy I've been seeing thinks I'm crazy. He's the polar opposite of Ransom." I struggled to picture the fair-haired boy I'd seen her with inside. "He asked me out forever until I finally ran out of reasons not to say yes," she added, as if I'd voiced some disapproval. Then she asked, "How are you holding up?"

"I'm all right," I replied with the last of my energy. Drifting, drifting, falling backwards. I shifted my left leg back a pace and established a new center of gravity.

"I keep wondering about the journal," she said. "I know it would tell us so much about him."

I was either about to reply or tumble down the hill when we were interrupted by Matt's anxious yell. "Is that you, Fin? Fin, is that you?" As he approached us and realized that it was, in fact, me, Fin, he panted, "We have to get out of here. A bunch of Okies are looking for you." He was genuinely panicked and oblivious to the presence of a beautiful girl at my side.

"Okay, okay, Matt. I'm coming." I looked at Maggie with a blank expression that I knew did not convey the regret I felt at my inability to console her. "That's my ride," I explained, and did my best to walk a straight line to the parking lot.

As my bodyguards ushered me into the car, I noted how similar being high was with my state of mind since Ransom's death. I had moved slowly, sluggishly, in a cloudy funk, making an enormous effort to get through the days, unequal to the task of bridging the cloudy distance between the people around me and myself. Each moment I'd felt exactly as I had with Maggie: incapable of connecting.

By the time Phil shuttled us safely back to campus, I had sobered slightly. In the dorm, we changed and then Matt headed for the bathroom. On my way to join him there, I placed my hand on the knob I had not even looked at in weeks. I was surprised when it turned easily to the right, allowing me access to 219.

The palpable sense of his spirit in the air made me feel like a trespasser. After a moment's hesitation, I revisited his desk and dresser and rifled again through the empty drawers. I was more thorough this time, craning my arm awkwardly, making sure that my fingers explored every inch of the wooden terrain. I checked his closet in a similar manner.

As I turned to leave, my eyes were drawn to a crack in the plastic of the black floor paneling. I took a catcher's stance before it and pried at the brittle protrusion, a small section of which toppled to the floor exposing a hole in the green plaster wall. I reached my hand in as far as it would go but found nothing. Just dust and darkness.

"What are you doing?" Matt asked from the doorway, nearly giving me a heart attack.

"Looking for something," I replied.

❧

Phil Fercheck was true to his word. Sunday afternoon he appeared at our door bearing a hefty portion of his Eagles collection.

Panicked at the thought of being trapped with him, I said, "I was just on my way to the library, Phil. You're welcome to use my CD player, though."

"You're going to the library?" he asked, looking as if I had just shot his dog. "I'll leave something here for you to check out later, then."

I grabbed my jacket and the nearest stack of books and hurried outside. As I had no plans to set foot in the library — or any other place where I might run into vengeful Okies — I decided on a whim to pay a visit to the Pembrook Police in pursuit of Ransom's elusive diary.

The station house was a fifteen-minute walk from my dorm and stood adjacent to the Harrison Soccer Field. With modest brown brick walls and only one story, it looked more like an old-fashioned schoolhouse than a jail. I went through the single, Plexiglas door and found myself in the smallest lobby I had ever seen. For 'unauthorized personnel' like me the only option was to stand and wait at the sliding window. Within moments, an officer appeared behind the glass.

"Can I help you?" he asked.

I recognized him from the night of the suicide when he

had taken a seat beside me on my bed and asked questions. (Where were you when the gun went off? How many shots were fired? How well did you know the deceased?) His breath had smelled of Big Red. Then, as now, I stared at the tidiness of his sideburns, beard and mustache. They flowed together seamlessly: an immaculate red pretzel of hair atop his long Irish face.

"I'm not sure," I replied. "I was a friend of Ransom Seaborn's…"

I didn't know how to proceed, how to word anything. I hadn't anticipated actually speaking with anyone.

"I remember you," he said gently, a tiny smile of concerned recognition creeping into his lips. "Dan, isn't it? What can I do you for?"

Hearing his questioning voice again sent a shiver up my spine.

"I was just wondering if you guys found anything unusual in Ransom's room that night. I know he didn't leave a note but he used to write all the time in an old brown journal, and I haven't been able to track it down."

"No, Dan," he said, shaking his head and rubbing his well-groomed chin. "We searched that room pretty good. There was hardly anything. Some clothes and a few books, but nothing like what you describe." His face became thoughtful. "Of course, there was that poem."

Poem? This was the first I'd heard about a poem. "Yeah," I said as if I remembered it all perfectly. "What was that?"

"From what I gather, it was something his mother had written. Hand-written original copy. Apparently, she was a pretty big time writer. Of course you could hardly read it with all the…" He opted against the use of the 'b' word. "You say he kept a journal?"

I could tell he was a talker from the way he leaned in, tilted his head, earnestly posed his question. An easy-going, good-natured lover of conversation who would gladly spend the better part of an afternoon discussing a journal nobody had found.

I, on the other hand, was not. "Yeah," I replied. "Thanks anyway."

I debated returning to my room but decided it probably wasn't safe yet, so I headed to the diner for a late lunch. I kept wondering about that poem as I went. What was it? Had he had it all along? Was it an old friend he'd brought out to witness his last journey or had it just come in the mail that day?

The post-church rush was thinning in the diner, and I took a seat at the white counter. Stella, the grinch-woman, appeared before me bearing a brown-lipped pot and blocking my view of the fresh-pie display case.

"Coffee?" she asked in a voice deeper than the one I remembered. Either she had a cold, or menopause and puberty had more in common than I realized. I nodded and she poured the steaming liquid into a cup. "Anything else?"

"Chicken sandwich and fries," I replied.

I was surprised to hear Maggie's voice amidst the confusion behind me. Glancing over my shoulder, I saw her sitting at a table across from a thin, bespectacled girl with straight brown hair. The table was littered with the remains of their meals, and strewn with opened books and notebooks. I was relieved when Maggie smiled and came over. After my Rocky Balboa routine the night before, I thought she might have given up on me.

"Mind if I join you for a minute?" she asked, sitting on the stool to my right.

"Not at all," I replied, eager for the opportunity to speak to her in multi-syllables. "I'm actually glad I ran into you. Sorry I had to leave like that last night. My roommate's a little up-tight."

"It looks like you made it back safely," she remarked, checking me for bruises. "I wouldn't worry about the Okies, Finbar.

They're too close to losing their charter to do anything crazy." She glanced at my book. "What are you reading?"

"The Mill on the Floss."

"Mabry?"

"Yeah." After an awkward pause I continued, "Did Ransom ever show you a hand-written copy of one of his mom's poems?"

"No. Why?"

"The police found it in his room," I explained, failing to mention that I had too but couldn't remember. Maggie slowly shook her head, deep in thought. "I searched his room for the journal again last night," I continued. "It's disappeared. He must have tossed it. Or maybe his father has it after all."

"I doubt it, Finbar. It's gone. He probably did something dramatic like burn it or something." We were interrupted by the appearance of surly Stella who deposited my food and refilled my coffee before bulling away. "It was just comforting to think there was a part of him out there still," Maggie added. "Waiting to be found. Like he's not all gone yet."

"You never know," I offered unconvincingly.

"No, you never know," she echoed. "Well, Finbar, I'll let you eat. Thanks for the update."

As she stood to leave I said, "Sorry if I bummed you out, Maggie."

"No," she assured me. "I'm glad we talked. Thanks, Finbar."

When I got back to the room there was a note on our door in Matt's distinct scrawl. 'Steve called AGAIN! He wants to know if you're going to Ronny's party. P.S. Thanks for abandoning me.'

Ronny's party. Another thing to dread. I got into bed and slept until midnight.

❧

Monday afternoon I followed the routine I had established over the preceding weeks. I went to the library and worked on assignments into the early evening, then hit Block just before it closed and ate a quick dinner. I stopped by my room and picked up the novel-of-the-moment, then sat in the Jefferson stairwell reading until I grew bored and relocated to a rehearsal space in the Fine Arts Center. At eleven, I went to the Podunk, read and drank coffee for an hour before the lights went out at midnight.

Long, late-night walks were the prime diversionary tactics I employed against my nemesis, sleep. The weather had not yet turned and Pembrook was the kind of place where you could stroll at any hour without fearing for your safety. My walk that night took me along the slanting, intersecting streets of the town's soft underbelly. Small, tidy backyards overlapped behind narrow clapboard houses. Every vertical surface was painted white.

On my way back to campus, I stopped by Mister Donut. Fay, the gregarious, gray-haired sweetheart, worked the late shift as if she were hosting a talk show. She greeted me as I stepped through the doorway. She wore a limp, peach uniform that matched the wall paint, and an un-starched white apron.

"What are you doing out so late, Danny?"

She always asked me the same question upon arrival, always with the same motherly concern. It had never changed in the dozen or so other times I'd stopped in during her shift, though it was only recently that she had managed to pry my name from me.

Standing at the register, before the well-stocked shelves of fresh donuts, I made my habitual reply, "Just walking."

"You and your walking," she remarked. "You're gonna burn holes in your shoes. Regular or decaf?"

"Regular," I said as I took my usual seat. For the moment I was Fay's only studio guest.

Before we could launch into our usual lightweight banter, I glanced out the front window and caught sight of Ransom's elderly chess partner—wearing the same jean jacket, the same plaid cap—shuffling in the distance down Main Street. I threw down a dollar and hurried out the door, apologizing to Fay as I went. He was out of my sight but I ran to where he'd been, hoping to pick up his trail. Standing outside of The Strand Theater, I glanced up and down the deserted sidewalk. The portly old man was nowhere to be found.

I don't even know why I wanted to speak with him. Maybe to be sure he was flesh and blood and not some ghost sent to lure Ransom to the other side. Or maybe to be certain he had heard about his rival's death. Or possibly just to learn about the friend I didn't know.

❧

After classes Thursday, I sat against a tree near Siberia and fumbled with the lid of my large coffee. The spot was strategically chosen: off the beaten path, yet out in the open enough so as not to be easily ambushed. Maggie's appraisal of the Okie situation had eased my mind somewhat, but why push the issue?

A shadow fell across me and I looked up to see Dr. Exley looming over me, effectively eliminating the sun from my world. So much for ambush-avoidance strategies: I could not have been more surprised if a giant Holstein had come over and struck up a conversation.

"Daniel Finbar," he said, casually tossing his books down and seating himself atop the dirty roots. "Daniel Finbar," he repeated, seeming to derive great pleasure from the sound of the words.

"What's up, Dr. Exley?"

"Your name came up this morning," he divulged. "My colleague, Dr. Mabry, says she's worried about you."

I was flabbergasted that these two professors even knew my name, let alone discussed my well-being.

"Why is she worried?" I asked.

"She says you're withering away right before her very eyes. She's poetic like that. Come to think of it, though, you do look a little peaked." He paused theatrically and looked me up and down. "Well, what do you have to say for yourself, Daniel Finbar? Is there any truth to these allegations? Are you withering away right before our very eyes?"

He emphasized each word, as if he couldn't choose an anchor, as if they were all just too damned important to the question. I didn't answer. I didn't even know if he expected me to. When he resumed speaking, his voice had turned softer, conspiratorial.

"I don't like giving advice, Daniel. I mean, what do I know? I'm a professor at Harrison College for God's sake." He could somehow speak and laugh simultaneously, the embodiment of self-deprecation. "But here goes anyway.

"When you're eighteen," he began, "—you are eighteen, aren't you?—everything is utterly enormous, and I am talking colossal. When am I going to get laid? What am I going to do with my life? Why doesn't anybody understand me? What is the meaning of that Pink Floyd lyric?" He paused, grabbed a rock and chucked it about three feet, then added, "Why did my friend, Ransom Seaborn, have to kill himself? The thing is, and this is what you would call the crux of my argument, everything, and I do mean everything, passes. Pain diminishes. I promise. The world may look all jumbled up and ugly to you now, but some day, maybe tomorrow, maybe ten years from now, things will unjumble...or at least you'll forget why you ever wanted them to."

I nodded, pretending to understand. He gathered his books and lifted himself up. "That's all." As he walked away, he turned and said, "I know you didn't hear a single word I said, and that's all right."

I stayed there alone, sipping my coffee.

❧

That night I dreamed a dream I would have often that first semester. A paratrooper floated through the air, his chute pulled. A crowd of people gathered around a chalk marked bulls-eye in a clearing below, but he floated away from it. It seemed he was heading for disaster, towards a treetop or the whirling blades of a helicopter. He was moving in the wrong direction, and could never possibly land on the bulls-eye.

Gradually, I made out the paratrooper's face as he floated through the sky. It was Ransom, his eyes closed, his head tilted and resting on his chest. I was a child, running from the expectant crowd, running to where I thought that he would land so that I could save him. I ran, and I ran, down through the landscape of my childhood, down through the school yard, past our house and across our dead-end street, down along the path behind Dunn's house, into the fields where the Eldridges grew tomatoes and rhubarb and where we were forbidden to go. I stared desperately into the clear summer sky, but had lost him. I woke up with my neck sore from looking upward in every direction, trying to find Ransom in the sky of my dreams.

❧

My paper on the Russian Revolution was a solid effort, though hardly a brilliant one. I finished it in the main room of the library at 10:37 Friday night. With no pressing social engagements, I decided to use the final twenty-three minutes before closing to pay a visit to dear old J.D. Salinger, my favorite literary recluse. It had been over a month and I was due for a dose of Holden Caulfield's world-weary humor.

I went upstairs and gazed across the now familiar titles: *Raise High the Roofbeam; Carpenters; J.D. Salinger Revisited; The Catcher in the Rye.* Something was different. Studying the shelf more closely, I determined what it was: tucked between *Franny and Zooey* and *Nine Stories* was the faded brown notebook I had given up for lost. I pulled it from the shelf, half expecting an alarm to go off and campus security to come rip it from my trembling hands. Stunned, I went to sit at the desk where I'd first seen Ransom Seaborn and turned to the last page of his journal.

❦

I bet you were hoping I'd get to the journal around now. Almost there.

"*Ever had a lousy blow job?*"
This unexpected question came from Lazy-eyed Lou as I passed the office this morning. It was warm enough that neither of us needed a winter coat. I knew there was a punch line I could offer, something about pizza maybe, but I remained silent. As it turned out, Lou wasn't joking, he was curious.

"*Have you ever had a lousy blow job?*" *he repeated, his mouth a round donut of inquisition, his torso bobbing slightly, rhythmically.*

"*Not lousy, I don't think,*" *I answered.* "*Maybe sub-par.*"

"*Hey, a package came this morning,*" *he said. My too-technical answer had bored him instantly. He handed me the large, padded envelope.* "*You moving in, or what?*"

I called Joel Seaborn two nights ago, my first night here. He answered after three rings.

"Finbar?" he asked. "Dan Finbar? Is that really you?"

I was relieved he even remembered who I was. "Yeah, Joel. It's me."

"What are you doing? How have you been?" He spoke to me as if I was a long-lost brother who'd been presumed dead only to show up at the front door. "God it's good to hear from you, Fin. What have you been up to?"

I had carefully planned my answer. I focused on my musical career and gave him the Reader's Digest version of my five-year rise from Pittsburgh's solo acoustic open stages to the plush RCA conference room in which we signed our big deal. I told him about the songs I'd written, my band mate brothers and some of the more notable gigs we'd played. I poured all of my scarce energy into sounding positive and upbeat, not wanting him to sense even a trace of my sorrow. I didn't mention drinking or Maggie or anything that might betray emotion, for fear it would hinder the success of my mission.

"I have a favor to ask of you, Joel," I said when it felt like the conversation was winding down.

"Anything, man."

"This is kind of strange," I began, "but I was wondering if you could photocopy Ransom's journal entries for me and send them to this motel I'm staying at."

The concern I'd feared appeared instantly. "Why are you staying in a motel, Dan?"

"Writing songs for our next record," I lied, glancing at my gun. "You know? Kind of getting away from all of life's distractions."

Our exchange ended with him taking down the address of the Cloverleaf and promising to get a package in the mail the next day. Overnight. Of course, he kept his word.

Music, for me, was a mysterious and beautiful woman with whom I fell in love when I was fifteen years old. As is the case with the truest romantic loves, our relationship evolved over time into something deeper. The 'squealing feeling' remained, but there were layers and layers beyond and beneath. She supported me when nothing else could; understood me when no one else did. A lyric, a melody line, the indefinable energy of the most transcendent recordings — these were the salves I used to heal my wounds.

My performance career began in college. Early in my junior year I formed an acoustic duo with a classmate from Buffalo named James Diener. We played a few originals, but stuck mostly with the Grateful Dead covers people couldn't seem to hear enough of. We got a steady gig at an off-campus bar and became pseudo-celebrities in the bubble that was Harrison College.

By the time graduation rolled around I'd decided to chase my muse, a choice based as much on job-interview phobia as on artistic compulsion. I moved back home and worked on my writing. I spent countless hours recording new songs on my basement four-track, the results, replete with numerous overdub harmonies, a cross between the Beach Boys and Bob Dylan, sans the visionary genius. (I remember, though, the exhilaration that accompanied the writing and recording of the first song I knew was good. 'People Change' it was called…its power emerging more with each new reading. This is what I'm meant to do, I knew finally.)

I began frequenting local open stages and trying out my stuff. Gradually, I became part of the Pittsburgh music community. I made a name. I found a band. I found another band. I found the right band. We began touring and recording and gathering steam. All the while I was finding my voice, both literally and lyrically. Themes began to emerge. Characters appeared and reappeared. I began to see myself as a spokesman for those on the brink: between heaven and hell; lust and loneliness; God and nothingness; love and loss. People responded.

By the time we put out our second record, our sales were strong enough to garner the attention of several record companies. After some considerable wooing by RCA records, we inked a deal and were *on our way. We played our last gig for two thousand fans in the Chicago House of Blues the night before Thanksgiving, less than a month ago.*

Joel's friendly note reads, "Great to hear from you, Fin. This time don't wait so long between calls."

I hear the soft pitter-patter of raindrops on the window. A white Christmas looks unlikely. I'm sitting here hypnotized by Ransom's tiny script, amazed by how easily it transports me to that night long ago when I made my discovery and ran to show Maggie.

Chapter Five

My mind raced as I left the library and ran across campus to the Margaret Esther Pugh dormitory. I assumed Maggie lived there, as it housed the majority of senior women. The lobby was grand and stately, the usual Protestant austerity forsaken for Victorian excess. A staircase spiraled up from the sparkling sea of marble on which I stood. I studied a list of the hall's inhabitants and ascertained Maggie's room number.

"252," I said to the middle-aged woman who sat behind the desk where visitors came to 'buzz' desired residents.

She called the room and after listening for a moment said, "No one answers. Do you want me to try someone else?"

"No, thanks," I replied, ready to cease my mission until the following morning. But then I saw the girl with whom Maggie had been studying at the diner. She sat on one of a half-dozen plush velvet couches in the elegant study.

"Excuse me," I said as I approached her. "Do you know if Maggie's around?"

"Who wants to know?" she asked.

"Dan Finbar," I answered.

"Jessica Newman, Dan Finbar," she replied. "How do I

know you won't just haul off and punch her in the face? I'm very protective of my roommate. Did Sully track you down yet?"

It took a moment for the question to register. Sully must have been the burly red-coat I'd decked six nights before.

"Not yet." I fingered the worn journal in my hand and asked again, "Is Maggie around? I just buzzed her but she didn't answer."

"She's here somewhere, Dan," she replied. "Let me run up and find her for you. Don't beat anyone up while I'm gone."

In Jessica's absence, I studied the red patterns—pencil thin outlines of Harrison's finest architecture on the milk-white porcelain china in the cabinet against the wall. My heart was still racing.

"What's up, Fin?" Maggie asked as she reached me, her expression a mixture of surprise and concern. I turned to her, revealing my precious cargo. The rosiness drained from her cheeks as if she had seen a ghost. She sat on the sofa and pulled me down next to her. "Where'd you find it?"

"Under J. D. Salinger in the library. I think he knew I'd see it there eventually."

"Did you check the end? Did he leave a note?"

"The last pages are torn out. The final entry's from the day before he died."

She took it from my hands, rubbed the smooth exterior, lifted it to her nose as if inhaling Ransom's cigarette scent. "Let's go somewhere," she said. "I'll go get my keys."

❧

We rolled out of Pembrook in her gray '78 Impala, a recent hand-me-down from her older brother, she explained. We passed the Bi-Lo, McDonald's, the gun shop and Ice Cream Shack. The 'Welcome to Pembrook' sign receded in the rear view mirror as we breezed by the entrance to 79 and into the less populated Merker County back roads. Maggie's fingers were white as she clutched the steering wheel. At red lights and stop signs, she glanced over at the journal resting on my lap as though it might turn into Ransom at any moment and complete his resurrection. A rich female voice sang soulfully through the car's speakers, something about love and affection.

"Who are we listening to?" I asked.

"Joan Armatrading."

"I've never heard of her. Sounds good."

"I saw you in the talent show, Finbar. You were great."

We spent the next ten minutes engaged in small talk. I learned that Maggie was from Erie—the 'armpit' of Pennsylvania as she described it—the second of three kids. Her older brother, Brian, landscaped for a living and was loud and good-natured. Deanna, the rebellious seventeen year-old, was the only one still living at home.

"She lives with my dad and his lovely new wife."

"I take it you don't like her."

"She's all right," she clarified. "It's my dad I could do without. I think my mom brought out the tiny bit of good in him and when she died his true self came out."

At a flashing yellow light she made a right. The turn signal clicked loudly, then cut out as our path straightened.

"So what are you going to do with your life?" I inquired. "You graduate in May, right?"

"All I know for sure is that Jessica and I are backpacking through Europe next summer. After that, I'll probably go to grad school. My ultimate goal is to be a high school English teacher."

"I love to read," I said. "Ever since Ransom, it's all I do, pretty much."

"Have you been to Stonewall?" she asked. "It's a great little book store in town. It's right behind the bank. I go there most Saturday mornings to read and drink coffee. How about you, Finbar? What's your life's ambition?"

"I'm not sure," I replied. "Maybe something with music. I can't really picture myself in a suit and tie. Who knows? I'll probably end up being an accountant or something."

Postponing our descent into the world of Ransom's mind, we filled the silent spaces with more small talk, gathering our strength and shoring our defenses.

We pulled into the Landmark Hotel, a broken-down barn of a bar, home away from home for some of the less motivated upperclassmen. I would come to know it intimately myself, later. The parking lot was nearly full. We found a corner spot that suited our purposes, being removed from the flow of patrons entering and exiting the building. The street light next to us provided enough light for reading.

"I'm gonna grab a six-pack," Maggie said, opening the door. "Have a preference?"

The situation definitely called for a drink. "Anything's fine," I replied.

She returned five minutes later, carrying a brown paper bag from which she produced a carton of six Budweiser bottles. "It's packed in there," she said, waving off my offer of cash to help pay for the beer.

Warm air wafted through our cracked windows. It felt like springtime, in spite of the fact that it was almost November. I sat Indian style, facing her, on my side of the big front seat. We opened our beers and drank from them. I placed the cold glass container on the floor at my side, wiped the condensation from my hands onto my jeans, and opened Ransom's journal.

He had printed in neat, tiny letters. Occasionally, a word was scratched out, with parentheses placed around it, but overall it was surprisingly clear and error-free.

"Ready?" I asked and she nodded, staring straight ahead, braced for anything. I cleared my throat and read aloud:

September 1
I begin this at the start of my Sophomore year. It's my first journal; an attempt to bring order to the chaos of my mind, scratch at the core of my being, kill time.

This moment finds me frozen in sunlight, a stranger in a strange land. I'm falling into easy isolation again. The smiling-faced people pass me like so many servants in God's palatial country estate. I see them through the stained glass window. I see them through squinted eyes, children like myself, but not like me. And not like each other, of course, either.

Me, me, me, who is me? The only child of a deceased poet and her devoted alcoholic husband? The sad writer-in-waiting who stutters silent soliloquies all through the days and nights, a self-proclaimed ostrich in a merciless world of swans? The son who couldn't meet his father's eyes when we parted ways not two hours ago, afraid of what I might see there, afraid of what he might see in return? The numb-assed freak, sitting too long, waxing phlegmatic on the library steps with evening approaching and morning long since gone?

September 2
Why do I stay silent when their greetings issue forth? Why do I not respond in kind to their pleasantries and salutations? The answer is the invisible "I don't know" that glues my bones and blood together somehow, magically, irreversibly, making me a ghost. And that is what I am now: the Ghost of Harrison College.

Yet the sky grows more beautiful each day. Now it is purple, now it is pink, glowing pink from within its swirling layers of ruffled clouds, glorious pink feathers of the eagle that is the sky. Now purples and whites, mellow and majestic.

"God this is weird, Finbar," Maggie blurted. "Hearing his words again. Hearing him talk like that. Hearing him call anything beautiful."

"I know," I agreed.

"It's freaking me out," she continued, her face lit up with wonder. "I mean, I really feel like he's in the car with us, just about to make his presence known. Or that your voice is going to turn into his. It's crazy. Look at me, I'm getting chills."

She lifted her arm to show me. Then she took another swallow of beer and nodded for me to proceed.

September 4

My first memory is of a crowded sidewalk in New York City. I was walking, reaching up for my mother's hand, surrounded by big people passing by and not looking down.

Next I hear her voice, soothing and lyrical, reading and reading to me. Stories in the morning, stories in the afternoon, stories all the time.

Four years old, she left me sitting on the living room floor, assembling Lincoln logs. It was snowing out. She left the door open, snow and wind blew into the entryway. When I realized I was shivering, I went to the window and saw her walking up to the front door. She wore the robe she'd left the house in, five, ten, fifteen minutes before. Snow blanketed her black hair and her feet were bare. She never told me where she'd gone.

"Did he talk much about her?" I asked.

"Just what he said that first day. About the poem, and her dying. Did he tell you anything?"

"He said she was crazy and that he thought he might be following in her footsteps. He talked about her reciting poetry for her friends when he was a kid. He had her picture above his bed. Right beside yours."

"I never made it into the inner sanctum," she remarked. "What did she look like?"

"It was kind of hard to tell. The picture was old, black and white. It was from the jacket of her first book. She looked a little like him, I guess. Dark hair, dark eyes…dark everything. She was pretty." I took a deep breath. "Ready?"

"Yeah."

At the age of seven I flew with her across the ocean to a poetry conference in the south of France. She wore a white summer dress. Our giant airplane touched down in Paris. A train took us to the town of Angouleme. We were greeted at the station by two smiling Englishmen and transported, luggage and all, in a boxy white truck to a 13th century castle, Merrouatte. My mother kept saying how exhausted she was, but she didn't look exhausted. She looked lit up inside, and smiled like an angel, and everyone seemed to want to make her smile, including me. I was jealous of them all. But my jealousy dissolved as I discovered the world of Merrouatte. All that week she worked and I roamed about the grounds amidst trees and stone walls, stone tables, stone chairs. A waterless moat surrounded the castle. I walked and walked for hours imagining Merlins and battlefields, battling evil dukes and kings who had me outnumbered, my back against the wall. "Open Sesame," I commanded the massive gates, and after a few terrifying moments, they did as they were told. Every night after dinner each poet recited his day's creation around the enormous, candle-lit table. My mother dropped her precious words like liquid pearls in our ears and I felt pride and adoration. We shared a lumpy King-sized bed. I fell asleep each night to her continuing saga of the boy with the butterfly net who roamed the French countryside searching for lost dreams. It was the happiest time of my life.

I looked up at Maggie and took a healthy swig of my beer. "Did Ransom ever mention an old guy he played chess with?" I asked.

"No." She turned to me, bending her right leg and tucking her foot under her left thigh. "Why?"

I told her about the day I'd followed him to the park and the strange sight I'd witnessed there. "They looked like old friends," I added. "I wondered if it was his grandfather or something."

"He never mentioned it. I like the image, though. Ransom in the park playing chess with a nice old man. You followed him?" she asked with a smile.

"I'm not above spying." I offered her the journal. "Mind taking over for a while?"

September 7

This morning I awakened thinking of Lizabeth, remembering the day that I met her, a Saturday. She stood by the lake and yelled out instructions to her workers on the water, her devoted canoeing instructors, the Dartmouth boathouse. I watched from a distance. I didn't even think of her age or my innocence or my looks or her availability. I just saw her there. Lizabeth the siren. Lizabeth the sage. Lizabeth the chesty altruist. My silence was no routine, I was terrified and shivering. She walked over to me. You're not supposed to swim here. What's your name? All the usual bull shit. The first woman since my mother I felt affection for. We fucked on her sofa two days later. She warned me of the sadness sex brings. I didn't tell her that sadness was no longer a word for me, it was me. She went away not saying if she'd return. She didn't like the way I made her feel. She cursed my inwardness. I pissed her off. I said good-bye silently.

"It's scary to hear how detached he could be. He sounds so cold," Maggie said. I sat silently, blushing internally, embarrassed by Ransom's bluntness.

Maggie continued.

And now I sit at a desk on the second floor of the library, far removed from the bustling crowds down below. Gradually my autonomy reasserts itself and people leave me be. To be or not to be, that is the question. Is it better to shun the advances of well meaning strangers, or pretend to engage, pretend to listen, pretend to have energy, or empathy, or anything? The choice is mine. My father calls and speaks in a weary voice, more alone than ever now. What does my voice sound like to him?

September 9
I wasn't always like this. As a young child, four-five-six, I fought self-consciousness with all my might. It crept in long before she left us, though. The blue black melancholy. The gaping awareness of not fitting in, of being lost. I started thinking too hard before I said things. If I meant it to be funny, I said it a hundred times inside my head before speaking it aloud. Maybe it was because I never knew what to expect

from moment to moment. Would she be crying soon, even though she laughed? Would she recognize me when she awakened from her afternoon nap? Am I turning into her? Does her voice speak through me now? How long can I go without talking?

When things were good, they were very good. Weeks and months went by in peace. At least that's how I remember it. She waited with me at the bus stop singing softly always. I imagined her making up rhymes and poems as I walked from class to class, brave little infidel. She greeted me warmly on my returns. Evenings, they walked behind me, holding hands, talking. When things were good, they were downright blissful.

My dad says you're only as sick as your secrets. I second that motion. Our secrets define us. They tell us who we are. My secrets talk to me every damn day.

September 10

Third grade overcast February afternoon, Valentine's day. My energy combined with my ambition to overcome my cowardice as I wrote the sweet rhyme for Jill Schiller, the long necked, golden haired, girl across the room, school girl of my dreams. "Roses are red, violets are blue, I'll be your Valentine, will you be mine, too?" Out of my hands I instantly regretted my impetuous advance, retreating to my familiar uncertainty, staring down through the green floor. She walked slowly toward me, through the crowd of last period partiers, through the sea of candy and cards being bandied about, she stood before me, two feet in front of me, "I don't want to be your Valentine." She smiled. She liked her power. Could she really have been so cruel?

God is a weekday comic strip, once in a blue moon he's funny, but no one ever reads him anyway.

The silence in the car caught me off guard. I had fallen under the spell both of Ransom's words and Maggie's voice. The parking lot came to life as those who had just closed the bar drunkenly searched for their vehicles or made final pitches to potential overnight guests. It was after two am.

"I asked Ransom if he believed in God," I announced.

"What did he say?"

"Something about there definitely being a God, but that he was unknowable...that was the word he used."

"What do you think?" she asked, surprising me a little.

"I think God's knowable...or maybe feelable, but not really describable. So it's all right to think about Him and pray and everything, it's just not worth talking about. It's beyond talking."

I was semi-impressed with my philosophical stand. I had never expressed these thoughts before and thought they had a nice ring. Maggie wasn't buying it.

"What are you guys afraid of?" she asked. "What's so bad about talking things through, or thinking out loud, even if you can't describe something, or it is unknowable?"

"What do you believe?" I asked.

"All sorts of things. I believe in God. I believe in heaven. I believe there are angels in each of us and that we can become them if we want to."

"But don't you think God is a mystery?" I asked. "I mean isn't that almost part of the definition?"

"I guess, Finbar," she said unconvincingly. "But it's a mystery worth solving, or at least talking about."

She handed me the opened journal.

September 13

Everybody looks familiar. Have I finally seen all the prototypes? Hey you, hey you passing by, you were in my kindergarten class. You were in my tenth grade English. You lived two houses down from me when we were kids. Everybody looks familiar.

September 16

This afternoon I walked into town to buy smokes in the cigar store. I met a man there who introduced himself as 'Old John.' He asked me if I had a minute and invited me to sit with him on the park bench just outside the shop. The day was hot, but he wore a jacket and a cap. We sat there together and lit up, he a pipe, me a cigarette. "They tell me you're a chess player," he said.

Who 'they' were or how 'they' knew I played chess I did not know, but they were right. My father had taught me. "Yes, I do," I replied, going with the flow, another lesson of my father's.

"Meet me next Tuesday in the park on Elias and we'll see what's what."

I think I'll go. I will go.

The good Lord willing. And if the creek don't rise.

"There's your old chess player," Maggie said. "God, Finbar. This is so bizarre. Don't you think this is bizarre?"

I nodded.

"I just can't believe he had this secret life, and that he expressed himself so well...and that he had a chess partner. Don't you find it all bizarre?"

"It's bizarre," I said, afraid she might assault me if I didn't agree. "Although it kind of makes sense that Ransom's only college friend would be an old man he played chess with. Keep going?"

"Keep going."

Old John's ploy reminds me of the only vacation we ever took, to Orchard Park, Maine. They sat on their blanket on an empty stretch of beach, early, before the crowds arrived. I played alone, dressed in my cowboy clothes, packing a silver cap pistol in my brown leather holster tied above the knee. My parents glanced at me between sections of their books. Then it happened, I saw him approaching from twenty feet away, a six year old pistolero like myself. We instinctively knew what must happen. We faced off in the harsh morning sunlight, dangerous strangers, in a life and death showdown. We drew simultaneously but I shot first and dove sideways. The battle that ensued was inconclusive. My parents watched, smiling.

September 18

Yesterday I sat and watched a blade of grass for two hours. I was sad to surrender to the darkness. I stood on cramped legs, looking down still, on the blade I had chosen and with which I identified deeply. I am a blade of grass growing in spite of itself, wincing in the dogged sunlight, stuck in the dirt of it's random existence. I am the blade of grass waiting for the mower, greenly advancing through time. I almost cried at our parting. I saw it in dreams last night and see it still when I close my eyes. I am a blade of grass.

The passenger door opened. A large red arm reached in and pulled me out into the unseasonably mild night. Maggie screamed "No" as his fist made contact with the area just below my left eye. I fell to the ground, as he had fallen the week before. He kicked me once, hard in the gut, emptying me of wind and pride.

"Now we're even," he said, leaping into the back seat of his getaway car.

"Fucker," Maggie yelled, which struck me as funny, though I wasn't able to laugh at the time.

"Are you okay, Finbar? How many fingers?" she asked, kneeling beside me, flashing me the peace sign. She held my chin in her hand and studied my face and eyes. "We better get some ice on that."

We sped back, her rant alternating between Okie-bashing and Ransom puzzlement. Back on campus, she parked outside of Kessler, across from Jefferson, and guided me down into the rec hall. She left my side, then reappeared moments later with ice wrapped in a paper towel. We sat down at the nearest table. I was aware of our knees touching slightly, incidentally, and of the contact of our fingers as she handed me the makeshift ice pack.

"Do I look like a veteran prize fighter?" I asked.

She didn't answer the question. "Thanks for coming over tonight, Finbar. It really means a lot, you sharing this with me."

"Let's make a pact," I said. "Neither of us can read a single word of this journal without the other one present."

"You have yourself a deal."

"I'm going home tomorrow," I explained. "How about if we meet here Sunday night at eleven?"

"Works for me," she said as we stood to go. "Thanks again, Finbar. Take care of that eye."

She kissed me on the cheek and walked out the door.

❧

I am a blade of grass…

The words echoed through my sleep-deprived head until I whispered along with them.

…growing in spite of itself, wincing in the dogged sunlight…

I sat at my desk, remembering Maggie holding her ice to my face.

I am the blade of grass…

High from the beer and the discovery of Ransom's lost soul, his haunting meditation persisted.

…waiting for the mower, greenly advancing through time.

I don't know how long I sat there. But sometime in the midst of that short period of maybe fifteen minutes or so, and at that time when it's not yet day and it's no longer night, I swear I saw Ransom walking toward me from across the deserted quadrangle. I stood and looked closer as the lone figure disappeared.

Chapter Six

I thought, glancing in the mirror each time my pacing brought me past it, that I did look like a veteran prize fighter.

I had just returned from Saturday morning Accounting. My father would be arriving on campus any minute.

Matt stirred in his bed and I whispered, "Hey, Matt, I'm going home today. I'll be back tomorrow." I couldn't remember if I'd told him.

Matt removed the pillow from his face. Casting his near-blind gaze in my general direction, he said with a yawn, "Do you have a black eye?"

"I think it's actually bluish green," I replied.

"What happened?"

His tone suggested that I got black eyes at least once a week. I told him the story of the previous night's one-sided burst of violence, omitting the parts about Maggie, the journal, the Landmark and my sleepless night, and playing up my role as a defenseless victim.

"What a bastard," he said, fumbling for his glasses.

"The world's full of them, Mad Dog." Why I dubbed him that at that particular moment, remains a mystery. He wasn't exactly the 'Mad Dog' type. He didn't seem to mind, though. "There's my dad," I said, seeing our big red Bonneville crawling up the lane. I grabbed my laundry bag and made for the door. "See you tomorrow."

❦

My father thrived in enclosed environments where proximity was ensured and potential for escape non-existent. The car was his favorite. Once you were strapped in, he'd hit you hard with his deepest thoughts and 'level five' as he called it. Phrases like 'heavy petting' and 'mutual masturbation' might be tossed about for consideration. Seeing me there in the passenger seat, ten pounds lighter than when the semester started, with a scarred nose and a grossly discolored eye, there was no doubt that some 'level fiving' would occur on the long drive home. My only hope was to find a seam in the early, still-superficial, period of our talk and drift to sleep.

In response to his stares, I recounted the tale I'd just spun for Matt, adding the chapter from the previous weekend. I then closed my eyes, pretending to slip away into the land of dreams.

"Danny," he said gently, minutes later. "Dan." He shook my arm with his right hand, rousing me from my false slumber. "Do you think we could have a little talk?"

Of course we could. I was trapped. I sat up reluctantly and angled to face his profile.

"Your mother and I are worried about you, Dan. You're a different person since going to Harrison. Look at yourself. You're not eating. You hardly talk. You're all banged up." He paused. I stared at the cars on the opposing highway.

"I want to make a suggestion, Dan. It's something I've thought a lot about, and I want you to keep an open mind. Okay? Why don't you drop out of Harrison and come back home, maybe go to Pitt next semester? We think it would do you good to get away from there, Dan. The money doesn't matter. We just want our son back safe. What do you say?"

Had he mentioned this idea twenty four hours earlier, before the return trip to Salinger and the journal pact with Maggie, I might have agreed. It might have looked like the best option: escaping the scene of my aborted friendship and returning to the tranquil stability of home life. As it stood, though, I felt I had something to discover at Harrison—some piece of the puzzle I could only find there now. Maybe it was about Ransom or maybe about myself. I didn't know.

"I don't think so, Dad," I finally replied, miles later. "I understand why you're worried and I know it's hard on you and mom, but this is something I have to work through on my own. I don't think running away would help anything."

There are times in the relationships between parents and children, brothers and sisters, husbands and wives, when a natural rift develops and there's nothing you can do but leave it be and let time work its slow, painful healing. Driving back to Pittsburgh on that warm October morning, my dad and I were as far apart as we had ever been.

"If you change your mind..." he said.

We made the rest of the trip in silence.

※

In that unexpected and spontaneous way some families have of gathering, we stood in our bright kitchen and decided to attend Mass that Saturday evening. Sara sat at the table finishing an Algebra problem. My dad walked in smelling of cologne, whistling as he straightened his tie.

I pulled a piece of left-over pizza from the refrigerator and bit into it as my older sister, Kim, who still lived in Pittsburgh, asked me about classes and the renowned Harrison strictness.

All of this followed a four-hour nap, a rushed shower and a conversation with my parents in which I informed them I'd be staying at Ronny's that night.

"Marcy told me they kick you out if you walk on the grass. Her brother went there." Marcy and Kim had adjoining cubicles at the insurance company where they both worked.

"How's Tom?" I asked. Tom, Kim's husband of three years, had lost his job in April and grown more despondent with each fruitless interview.

"Nothing yet," she answered, her brown eyes betraying her worry for a moment. "He has an interview Monday. Keep your fingers crossed."

The five of us left the house and went up into the half-filled parking lot. My father and Sara had privately warned Kim and me about a joke that my mother might be telling us. My mother had the endearing, if somewhat embarrassing, habit of hearing off-color jokes and relaying them to friends and family, often at inappropriate moments, completely oblivious to their true meanings.

"Kim and Dan, I have the cutest joke," she began as we climbed the steps into the church vestibule. We braced ourselves, and looked around to make sure no nuns or priests were in earshot.

"How does a Cub Scout become a Boy Scout?" she asked, as innocent as Pollyanna.

"I don't know, Mom, how?" Kim said, unable to resist playing along, struggling not to laugh.

"He has to eat a Brownie," she chuckled.

❦

It was my first Mass since Ransom died. I didn't pray. I didn't pay attention. I sat and I knelt and I stood without focusing. Father Tom spoke too long about something for his homily. I didn't listen. I offered no peace when the time came. Numbly, I ingested the pale, meaningless communion wafer and returned to our pew.

❧

I made the half-mile walk from the church to Ronny's house, down Vance and Frankstown and past the shopping center. Nothing looked the same as it had the summer before. Nothing was familiar any more. I was a stranger in my home-town: misplaced, displaced, out of step with my own life.

"Hey, killer," Ronny yelled, checking out my shiner through his thick glasses as he welcomed me.

"You should see the other guy," I said.

Ronny was in party mode. He had the house to himself and strutted ahead of me comically, the lord of his domain. Bone-rail thin and cleverly obnoxious, he was the guy the beach bully kicked sand on.

"I didn't know it was a theme party," I said, noticing his Hawaiian shirt, green Hawaiian lay, and straw hat.

"Everyone's downstairs," he said before opening the door that would lead us there. "Lisa's here."

It took me a moment to remember her. She had only been someone to talk about, a preoccupation borne of boredom and frustration. Her group of friends and my group of friends had somehow connected and joined frequently the summer before, to drink in basements, at drive-ins and in parks after dark. If she knew of my crush she never let on.

"Hey, dude," Eric Sebastian said, handing me a beer. "How's it going?" His twin brother, Scott, appeared at his side. Eric was a little thinner and parted his hair in the mid-dle, but if you didn't know them, you'd have trouble telling them apart.

"What happened to you?" Scott asked, his eyelids already heavy from drink.

I told them the story of the Okie lineman, my fifteen seconds of glory and his subsequent retaliation. Again, I kept the rest to myself.

"Finbar," Steve Clark bellowed, emerging from the bathroom and approaching from across the room. "You look like shit," he said, reaching our small circle. His curly brown hair was more unruly than usual, and one of his shirtsleeves was rolled up. By the looks of it, he'd been drinking a while.

"Nice to see you, too, Steve," I replied.

"Some fraternity fucker cheap shotted him last night," volunteered Mike Imuso, whom I hadn't even noticed until then. He stood 5'6", Hitler mustache and Beatle's hair, and leaned against a brown pole that connected the floor and ceiling. Mike was a fellow guitar player and music lover.

"You want me to go kick his ass, Fin?" Ronny asked, jumping into his fighting stance, his glasses slipping down his nose.

"Hi, Finbar," Lisa said, joining our discussion as her sister Karen and their best friend, Anita, listened. Lisa looked good. Her black hair was styled differently, straightened, down past her shoulders. She wore jeans and a tight red sweater that matched her lipstick.

"Hi, Lisa. How have you been?"

We did the drill. Pitt was all right, though she hadn't picked a major. Her parents were driving her crazy and she was hoping to get an apartment in Oakland with Karen.

"I overheard you talking about your eye," Lisa said. "Does it hurt?" She leaned closer than necessary to inspect it. I noted the irony of my situation. I had pined for her all summer and we hardly spoke. I barely even remembered her now, and she was flirting with me. Life was unfair on a lot of levels.

"Of course it hurts, he's a pussy," Ronny barked, startling

us all. And so began the taunting and instigating that defined and fueled us. With it returned the desperate commitment to reckless abandon that had overtaken us towards the end of the summer, when separation pended and sea changes filled the air. We were possessed, determined to hold back time.

Or, should I say, they were? Early on, I became an observer, even as I talked, laughed and drank. And, oh I drank, big, dying-of-thirst gulps, and those between 'ten counts' under the tap, and drainings of community pitchers.

"Who's up for quarters?" Ronny yelled, setting up a card table around which our motley crew converged. Lisa and I shared a seat.

"Remember when Mike Nicholas and Jeff drove up to the park with that fake siren on their dashboard?" Eric asked.

Lisa's leg was warm against mine.

"Yeah, I almost broke my neck running away," said Mike Imuso with a laugh, bouncing the quarter on the hard surface.

Her right hand rested on the outside of my thigh.

"Nice try, Mike. It's a bummer you suck so bad at quarters." Ronny was definitely the most adversarial of the game's players.

I felt a stirring in the crotch of my jeans.

"Don't forget he said that, Mike," Steve implored, worried that Ronny might escape justice if Mike got the quarter in the mug on his second attempt.

I planted my foot next to hers. Our calves pressed together.

"I remember my first beer," blurted Scott Sebastian to no one in particular, back for a moment from the brink of unconsciousness. Lisa smiled at the incessant banter as Mike sunk the coin and said, "Drink, Tweet."

'Tweet' was our nickname for Steve, who raised his arms dramatically in the air and groaned at the inhumanity of it all. He pulled the 8-ounce coffee mug towards him, lifted and emptied it saying, "I hope I catch a buzz soon." He was as drunk as I had ever seen him.

"I'm gonna go get some air," I said.

❧

I stood in the yard with my back to the house. It was typical of me to make an easy first move, then leave it for her to do the hard part: stand up and follow me out. The door opened and slammed and I turned to see not Lisa, but Mike Imuso emerging through the darkness.

"Sorry. It's only me," he said, reading my thoughts as he handed me a full cup of beer. "I don't know how much more I can take of Ronny." He turned away to relieve himself, the rules of etiquette suspended. "So how are you doing, Finbar?"

Mike and I had a rapport that went deeper than the time we'd spent together. Maybe it was our common love of music, or maybe it was the fact that he was funny and smart. I admired him.

"I'm not really sure, Mike."

"I heard about your buddy," he said. "How well did you know him?"

"Not that well, I guess. But he was the only person I really spent any time with up there." I paused, downing half of my beverage.

"You found him?" he asked, the first one brave enough to seek the hard facts.

"Yeah. Right after he did it."

A neighbor's dog barked, causing us both to turn our heads. A light rain began to fall.

"The weird thing is, I can't remember it. It's like I blocked out the whole scene. I can tell you what I had for breakfast that day, what I was wearing. But I can't tell you what I saw when I opened Ransom's door."

"No big surprise, man. Our brains know when something's just too much to handle," he said, echoing Dr. Sussman. "It'll come to you when you're ready."

I shrugged and sipped.

"I know this doesn't help much," he continued, "but I think shit like that just happens, man. We're not supposed to understand. People just do crazy things. People die."

I remained silent on the subject, thankful for the cover of the night. The door opened then and we heard Ronny and Steve doing a spirited rendition of *Hey Jude.* We looked back to see them framed in light, arms around each other's shoulders, swaying arhythmically.

"Assholes," Mike muttered, shaking his head as we moved to join them.

❦

'Quarters' became 'Euchre' which somehow evolved into 'Truth or Dare.' Ronny admitted that he'd cheated on a ninth grade exam (something he'd never told anyone). Eric sucked a shot of tequila out of Anita's cavernous belly button. Steve dared Mike to take his shirt off and consume a pitcher. Mike complied and instructed Steve to remove his pants. Ronny begged us all to join him in a moment of silence, in memory of the King, after which he stood and sang, *Can't Help Falling in Love.* By two a.m. we were all in stupors.

❦

I forget the pretext under which Lisa and I stumbled upstairs, drunken hobos in a William Kennedy novel. Beyond awkward, beyond drunk, we rolled on Ronny's parent's king-sized bed. I pawed at her breasts and tugged on the button of her black jeans. For a semi-conscious eighteen year-old virgin, I showed remarkable alacrity. We moved past passion, straight into bargaining.

She lifted my hands from her body to her lips and kissed my fingers.

I pressed my mid-section against her, hoping she would understand my urgency.

She whispered for me to relax, to slow down.

I guided her hand to my erection.

She searched for my eyes in the weak moonlight.

I willed her head down the length of my torso and her hand to the buckle of my belt.

She gave in to my blind, stupid longing, releasing me, and engulfing me with her mouth.

I lay in the darkness, waiting to come.

❧

I awakened on the bathroom floor, head pounding and mouth dry. I stood up slowly, took note of the painful stiffness in my back, and awaited the knowledge of how I'd gotten there. None came.

I splashed water on my face and walked down the hall to the bedroom. Lisa was gone. The bed was made. She must have left after I relocated to the bathroom floor. The clock at the Boyle's bedside showed 11:30.

I ventured downstairs and found Steve alone at the kitchen table reading the Sunday paper and drinking water.

"Where is everyone?" I asked.

"They all went to breakfast."

"When are Ronny's parents getting home?"

"Not 'till tonight."

"Did you see Lisa leave?"

"No," he replied. "What happened with you two?"

So began a system I would come to perfect in later years; a system in which I suppressed memories of less than fulfilling experiences by not giving words to them. My theory was if I don't tell anyone, then maybe it didn't really happen.

"I think I just passed out," I said, sitting down across from him. "How're you feelin'?"

"Not that bad," he replied, "I started drinking water at about one. That always helps."

Steve was one of those annoying drinkers who employed such tactics and had success with them. I, on the other hand, knew I would not recover from my hangover until Tuesday at the earliest.

"You know I've been trying to reach you at Harrison?" he asked in his gravest, most serious, future-lawyer voice. "I've talked to your roommate more than I've talked to you lately."

"I've been busy," I lied. "College is a big adjustment."

"I'm worried about you, Finbar," he replied. "We all are. Something's happening to you. You're like a different person almost."

"It's not that bad," I asserted. "I'll get it together. You don't have to worry about me."

I grabbed the paper's Leisure section and pretended to survey the front page.

"Well, what are you doing to get it together, Fin?" he asked, staring me down. "You don't talk to anyone. Your dad told me you won't see a psychiatrist or move home. Exactly what steps are you taking to get it together?"

"When did you talk to my dad?"

"Yesterday afternoon. You were asleep," he replied, his self-righteousness fading.

"Would you stop checking up on me, please? There's nothing wrong with me. Just give me some space for a while? Can you do that?"

"I'm only saying all this because I care about you, Fin," he said, the fight completely gone from his voice. "It's like you're unreachable all the sudden."

"I don't know what it is, Steve," I said. "I just can't seem to talk about it yet. Nothing's clear in my head. Sorry."

I left the room and went upstairs to shower.

Steve stopped me at the front door as I was leaving to go home. Reaching to shake my hand he instructed, "Call me when you're ready."

"I will," I promised.

🍁

I felt like the words 'BLOW JOB' were tattooed to my forehead, with the smaller cased post-script underneath: drunken and passionless. I was certain my dad stared right at it as he greeted me and said, "Any time you're ready, Fin." I could swear my mom leaned in to make sure she was reading it right when she brought my laundry up from the basement; and that sweet, innocent Sara mouthed the words of my scarlet badge before informing me of her plans to make the return trip to Harrison with us.

Pennsylvania's world famous potholes lulled me almost instantly to sleep. The standard, graphic images of Ransom's self-inflicted exit wound overtook my dreams. Only this time, the picture of his mother sprouted wings and she flew graceful circles around her lifeless son. Smiling, smiling, laughing, crying — tears of blood that covered his twitching corpse, forming a shell that cracked when I lifted it to my chest.

And then I heard screams, out of place, yet horrifying. I recognized them as belonging to me and opened my eyes to the terrified faces of Sara, my mom and my dad, who had pulled off the Turnpike to comfort me.

"Finbar," Sara pleaded, almost in tears, "what's wrong?" She had no concept of anguish and it broke my heart to be her instructor.

"I'm all right, I'm all right," I insisted groggily. I could see from their expressions they knew I was a liar.

❦

I took my late night stroll early that evening trying to shake loose from my lingering hangover. A fine mist drizzled on my hair and face. Shame festered in me from the night before, a weed growing in time lapse. I felt like a sponge in desperate need of wringing, soaked with impurities and sadness, and briefly considered calling Maggie to see if we could postpone our reading until the next night. My curiosity about our pending meeting won out, though. I stopped by my room and picked up the journal, then made my way to Kessler.

❦

I don't know which came first, the drinking or the emptiness. Maybe we inherit our penchant for boozing (or lack thereof) from one ancestor or another. Maybe we're all born with varying degrees of emptiness. Who knows? The fact is, even back then I was different. I took bigger sips...made bigger mistakes...had a bigger hole in my heart. Maybe I just answered my own question.

I remember my first taste of alcohol. It's one of my most vivid memories. I was eight years old. My father sat on the front porch sipping his Budweiser.

"You want a taste, Dan?" he asked, smiling playfully, holding up his half-filled glass.

I went to him, rested my hand on his knee and opened my mouth for him to pour in the mysterious liquid. It sent a warm shiver through me. When I asked for more he explained that I was too young to drink beer. He said beer was for grown-ups, not little boys late for bed. He tousled my hair and kissed me good night.

I rediscovered Budweiser — among other brands — near the conclusion of my junior year in high school and was amazed by its ability to eradicate inhibition. Girls once beyond my timid reach moved closer with each warm sip. My friends and I drank for courage and walked with a swagger we hadn't thought available to us. The warm spring nights became brilliant jokes to which we finally had the punch line.

How can something so sweet turn so ugly? How can the very thing that frees you turn into a prison?

You won't believe this, but the instant I wrote that last word, Lou knocked softly at my door.

"Can I interest you in a beer?" he asked, carrying in a six-pack of Rolling Rock.

"I'm on the wagon, Lou," I replied, amazed as ever by my cunning, baffling, invisible foe.

Chapter Seven

October 17

Nine…ten…eleven years old, summer camp New Hampshire, seven weeks away from home, relief and sadness. The hills and lake on display for the rich children, from New York mostly, miniature grown-ups complete with prejudice and hardened hearts. Junior A, Junior B. Cabin on the hill. The first bell rang each morning at 8:00. I'd awaken to Sal Russo's daily observation, "I got the biggest boner," as he marched off to the bathroom. The second bell rang at 8:25 and we appeared, sandy eyed, in the mess hall that always smelled of fresh paint. After we'd finished eating, and drinking our 'bug juice,' someone read yesterday's baseball scores to cheers of joy and horror. We looked at the chart on the porch to see our activities for the morning. The counselors liked me because I was quiet and did what they asked. That last year I kept so quiet they worried about me. A man named Ian, probably as old as I am now, thick and burly with hobbit hair and limitless energy, tried to reach me. He invited me to go on two mile runs with him, and went slow so I wouldn't give up. Some days he swam before the first bell rang. One morning I went with him. He didn't go to the part they'd marked off, though. He led me down a path and said, "I found the best place to swim, the water is warmer for some reason." I see him smiling, turning to say that, a towel around his neck, wearing only sandals and a bathing suit, "The water is warmer for some reason." He stripped on the shore throwing his things on the grass. "It's the only way," he said, casually, spitting out laughter. I did as he did and followed him in. Was it a fish or a branch I felt reaching around my waist? Was it a rock or a bottle I saw bobbing just beneath the water line? What ever it was I darted away from it, kicking and turning, running back along the buried path, stopping to dress just before the clearing. He didn't reach out to me any more after that. Later that summer, on visiting day, my father walked alone up the sun dappled hillside. "Your mom's not feeling so great," he said, seeing the light drain from my eyes and face. "Your mom says she loves you." "God, you are your mother's son."

Rosemary Gardner
Planted the seed of her doubt in me
She tilled the fertile soil of my dark imagination
Then left me to the fruits of her beginnings.

The *Star Trek* Gang surrounded the lit-up TV in the living room area and bashed the Klingons. Their linchpin, a tall, hunched, wise cracking bean sprout said loudly, "Oh yeah, like Kirk's gonna fall for that one," mocking his own enjoyment of the show.

His boys, four chain-smoking intellectuals, fellow freshmen I assumed, smiled knowingly. It was Tuesday, our third journal meeting, (fourth, if you included our trip to the Landmark) and the Trekkies had been there each night watching the eleven o'clock rerun on Channel 22.

Otherwise, Kessler Rec was deserted, the doors to the main

room where dances were held locked, the majority of freshman men drifting to slumber on the floors above. Maggie and I shared a square wooden table in the corner. We leaned side-by-side over the open book. To an observer, it would have looked as if we were studying for an exam.

Maggie wore her standard uniform: navy blue sweat pants, powder blue Mickey Mouse sweatshirt, white, low-top sneakers, which she took off the instant she sat down. Her hair was pulled back in a ponytail, held by a circular band, which she occasionally re-affixed, her hair falling free for an unguarded moment. She wore circular, brown-rimmed glasses and no make-up.

"What do you make of that?" she asked, halting the soothing murmur of her narration, keeping our pattern of stopping every few entries to comment or question.

"Sounds like Ian had a thing for little boys," I said. "And Ransom's mother is everywhere, in every line practically."

"Even then he was completely separate," Maggie noted. "Ten years old."

November 3

Nebraska.

Nebraska.

Go Bruce Springsteen, now you're cooking with gas. Your black and white cinemascope rolls through my head. It rolls and it rolls like a hot car, a massive old Buick with plates gone and no chance of eluding the authorities. It rolls like Kerouac's Midnight Ghost from San Fran to LA onward and onward to ecstasy. Rave on.

My dad didn't see it like I did. He traveled and went to
meetings. He didn't know she'd begun taking her pills with
wine and spending hours in the bathroom. I sat at home
wishing she'd leave the room or get out of the tub. I washed
her sheets and fixed meals she didn't eat.

November 13
What are they afraid of? Why are they trying so hard? Dr.
Phillips lectured us today on the evils of rock and roll music.
I couldn't fucking believe it. It promotes drunkenness and
drug-use and pre-marital sex he insisted. Is it 1955 here or
what? I ended up leaving the class. Chapels are bad enough
without being force fed this shit all through the day. There's
no 'Zen' in Presbyterian.

November 18
For her thirty-fifth birthday I gave her a thin collection
of poetry I had written called 'The Tidings I Bring.' I was
twelve years old. It contained ten poems in all and she read
each one aloud at our kitchen table after we'd brought out
her cake and before she had blown out the candles. I can still
see the late evening light seeping in through the windows,
combining with the flickering flames, transforming her eyes
into blue-gold torches. She lavished me with praise and said
it was the most perfect, personal, beautiful gift she had ever
received. She said she would treasure it always. I started to
cry for the perfect beauty of it all and she told me my tears
were gifts, too. Later that night I awakened to her screams as
she roamed the halls bellowing "Blake?"

Reading and discussing the journal stimulated me, kept
me from rest. I slept even less than before. I'd escort Maggie back to MEP, usually after midnight, and then walk off in
whichever direction caught my fancy, hoping to grow weary.

On Wednesday night, I walked along the main quadrangle, skirting the velvety rectangle of holy turf upon which we were forbidden to tread. As I approached the flagpole that stood across from Rockwell, I heard steps behind me.

"Finbar," Maggie said, out of breath as she reached me. "Wait up. Where are you going?"

"Long time no see," I joked. "I don't know, Maggie. I usually walk late at night to try and get tired. I haven't been sleeping too well."

"Mind if I tag along?" she asked. "I haven't been sleeping too well myself. It's hard to just turn off all the Ransom stuff and go to bed."

We crossed Stony Creek and followed the cement path to Main Street. As we passed the Strand I stopped and said, "About a week and a half ago I saw Old John walking right here." I pointed to a spot on the sidewalk. "It was about this same time. I ran over but he was gone. I wanted to make sure he knew about Ransom."

"It's such a small town," she said. "It shouldn't be too hard to track him down."

We reached the end of Main and I decided to show Maggie the cemetery Ransom had shared with me that first Saturday night. The tombstones, faceless in the moonless night, formed a dark silhouette.

"Ransom brought me here the first night we ever really talked," I said. "He was drunk. I'm sure he wouldn't have done it if he hadn't been. He said he came here to be with his mother."

Maggie moved closer to me. Our elbows touched through our winter coats.

"It makes me sad to picture him here all by himself," she said. "I wonder what he did when he came here. Did he talk out loud to her? Did he stand or sit? Did he cry?"

I explained how Ransom closed down after confiding in

me about his graveyard conversations. Maggie was all too familiar with the feeling of losing Ransom's company even as
his body remained present.

"Do you ever wonder what we're all doing here, Finbar?"
she asked as we continued walking. "You know—if there's a
purpose?"

"I try not to think about it," I answered.

"Oh yeah, I almost forgot. You're too cool to talk about
those things."

"I do wonder about it all, Maggie," I clarified, defensively.
"I just don't know anything. I sense things, I guess. I mean, I
feel God sometimes, and sometimes I get chills when I hear
a song or read a sentence or something, but I can't articulate
things myself, especially when I'm talking. So I tend to shut
down when these kinds of conversations come up."

"So you never talk about...about why you think we're
here?" she asked.

"I guess if I had to give an answer to that question, I'd say
we're here to learn things. I kind of like the idea that we're re-
incarnated over and over until we figure out everything we're
supposed to and then we're one with God. I'm pretty sure
that's not in the Catholic handbook, though."

"When my mom died," she said, "I kind of just gave up on
God. I went through a period where I was kind of like Ransom. You know? Real cynical and sad. That's probably why I
sympathized so much with how he was."

"How'd you snap out of it?" I asked.

"About two months after she died, I heard my little sister
crying late one night. I felt so sad for her. It finally got me out
of myself. I went in and sat on her bed and started saying all
the stuff my mother would have said. It's all in God's plan.
She's in a better place. She loved us so much. When I finally
went to sleep that night, I felt different. I believed everything

I'd just told Deanna. God, Finbar, I sure do get heavy around you."

"I kind of like it," I told her.

🍁

Fay smiled as we entered the brightly lit donut shop. As usual she asked, "What are you doing out so late, Danny?" This time she added a follow-up: "And who's your pretty friend?"

"Maggie," I answered, suddenly nervous.

"Hi, Maggie. I'm Fay." We sat at the vacant counter. Fay studied us a moment and said, "So, are you two an item?"

I felt as if I suddenly discovered I was naked. My face flushed. Maggie smiled, enjoying my discomfort.

"No, we're just friends, Fay. Thanks for asking, though." I was trying my best to maintain my composure.

"You know 'just friends' and 'an item' are closer than you think?" Fay pointed out. "I was just friends with my first husband until he knocked me up. Feeling dangerous tonight, Danny?" she asked, turning toward the coffee machine.

"Yeah, I'm feeling dangerous," I stammered.

"How 'bout you, sweetheart," she said to Maggie, "can I get you anything?"

"Same as Danny," Maggie answered, grinning openly.

By the time we left twenty minutes later, we had discovered that Fay's oldest son was a failure as a husband, as his father had been, and that Fay was giving serious consideration to having her hair dyed. Maggie's support of the move seemed to push her over the edge.

Standing outside Maggie's dorm for the second time that night, we laughed again at Fay's good-natured directness.

"I thought you were going to die on the spot, Fin. I didn't know you could blush like that."

"I wasn't that bad," I insisted.

"Thanks for letting me accompany you on your mysterious late night walk," she said. "We'll have to do this again some time. By the way, can we make it eleven thirty tomorrow night? I'm going to a movie with J.D."

J.D. So that was his name.

November 22

The thirteen year-old boy climbed through the open window. He stood in the yard basking in the moon-glow, savoring the faint breeze. He put on his jean jacket and tip-toed past his parent's room. He dug in his pocket for a stolen cigarette and the matches he'd grabbed at the Quick Stop when his dad wasn't looking. From that moment on, freedom would taste like nicotine and heaven would look like a quiet midnight street. Sweet relief from the rigors of sorrow. He heard the sounds of students laughing leaving late night bars. Summer time in Hanover. He looked both ways, then crossed over Haymaker checking to see if the Limegrover's lights were on, then walked down their driveway and on through their long back yard. He crouched and then slid down the steep dirt hill, using his feet for brakes, maintaining control of the body he could no longer control. At long last he stood by his calm destination, the Connecticut river. A sliver of moon reflected off the still surface. He breathed in, he breathed out. He breathed in, he breathed out. A great horned owl greeted him from the opposite shore. He took off his clothes and submerged himself in the cool, clear, crystal water. A nocturnal fish, a blissed out salmon, he wriggled free of worry, finally coming up for air. The thirteen year old boy repeated this process every dry night that summer, and sometimes when it rained.

December 7

Over and over I try to explain to myself in plain language the meaning of the bottomless pit inside my soul. It's been there all along, not just since the day she left. Despair is my junkie's salvation, it's my trusty addiction. Is she better off now? Did she need that release from her body? She'd sometimes be sitting on the porch when I awakened for school, and I felt like she had been there all night, just rocking and mumbling, sitting on the rocking chair she carried from the den. Where did she go when she left us like that? The same place she lives in now? She'd smile just a little when I squeezed her arm, helped her up, led her to bed. And then she'd wake up perfect, hours later, and stay with us a while. It got to where we never even thought about it. We ebbed and flowed right along with her. And when she shook free, it almost seemed like we were a normal family. She'd go to buy groceries, call up her artist friends, talk about writing. She'd ask me how school was and make plans with Dad to go to New York for their anniversary. She hardly shook free those last two years. She never shook free.

December 20

Here I go again, another Christmas with Dad. He'll load up on meetings. I'll load up on phantom sightings. I wish I could just stay here, sitting in this drab old room. I'd stare at the wall until it became my childhood, until it became her voice on Christmas eve, reading 'A Child's Christmas in Wales.' Oh, I could feel it then. The spirit of Christmas in flowing words and timeless images. She'd play with my hair 'till I slept.

Though the Pittsburgh Steelers made it a game for the first three quarters, by the fourth, the visiting Raiders had it firmly in hand. A knock at the door saved me from the sorry spectacle.

"Dan Finbar?" asked a guy I recognized from the floor below. I nodded. "There's a girl outside to see you."

"Thanks," I replied.

"Hi, Finbar," Maggie said as I stepped out the door.

"What's up?" I asked. We weren't due to meet for another eight hours.

"I was just wondering if you'd be up for taking a road trip to Erie with me," she began. "It's my sister's seventeenth birthday and my brother asked me to come home for dinner. Jessica has choir practice and I can't face my dad and the step wench alone. I'll have you home by eleven. I promise. We can take an extra night off from the journal."

We hadn't met since Thursday, having agreed that Fridays and Saturdays would be our nights off.

"Sure I'll go with you," I answered. "Let me get my coat."

I ran like a gazelle up to my room and rejoined her beneath the fading November sun.

🍁

Our ride along the interstate was pleasant, happily devoid of heavy conversation. I felt a palpable sense of relief sitting with her in broad daylight without the weight of Ransom's tortured psyche hanging between us. We were like school kids unsure of themselves when the teacher mysteriously leaves the room. "Do we start talking?" "Is she coming right back?" I rummaged through the tapes in her glove compartment and popped in the Joan Armatrading we'd listened to the night I found the journal.

Maggie recalled her first class with Dr. Exley, when, in the midst of an impromptu comedy sketch, he picked her to play the role of a femme fatale who inquires seductively as to what it will take to get an A in his class.

"He supplied my lines, of course, in some kind of mutated

Marilyn Monroe voice. And then he leaned down, 'till he was like an inch from my face, and whispered, 'Study.' I was mortified."

"So why didn't you get J.D. to go home with you?" I asked as casually as I could, saying his abbreviated name aloud for the first time.

"He has a big test tomorrow," she explained. "Plus, I need a friend more than a date at a time like this. My family can be a little abrasive."

❧

Maggie's sister was short and had straight, bleached blonde hair. She sat alone doing a crossword at the kitchen table, which was already set for dinner.

"I just farted," she said—the first words out of her mouth—as we entered through the back door.

"Happy birthday, Deanna," Maggie replied, visibly annoyed with her sister's poorly timed declaration. "This is my friend Dan Finbar."

My face must have been the color of the sun-ripened tomatoes that lined the windowsill. Like British royalty, the discussion of bodily functions was expressly forbidden in the Finbar household.

"Ah, Jesus," I heard someone proclaim from within the house.

"Maggie's home," Deanna shrieked.

"Your ass sucks canal water," the disembodied voice continued. "You wouldn't know a hold if it bit you in the ass."

"That's my dad," Maggie said, then led us to the living room.

"How ya doin', kid?" Mr. Stuard asked as we entered, only partially diverting his attention from the game. He sat sprawled out in a faded red recliner; an aging, leathery Paul Bunyan with beer can in hand.

Maggie's brother, Brian, lounged on the couch, his long frame covering its length. "Dad's talking to the TV again," he said.

"This ref doesn't know what the hell he's doing," their father continued. "Problem is, these guys work as lawyers and doctors all week when they should be studying football. They don't know what the hell's going on half the time."

"This is Dan Finbar," Maggie said, ignoring the astute observation. "He's a friend of mine from school."

"Nice to meet you, Dan," Mr. Stuard replied as I bent to shake his hand.

"I'd get up but I'm too hung over," Brian said.

"Real good, Bri," Maggie joked. "I bring a friend home and you can't even stand up to shake his hand."

"I already told you I was hung over," he said in mock indignation. "Here. At least I'll sit up and make room for you."

I took a seat beside Brian, who then elbowed me in the arm harder than I could have possibly expected and held out his hand to shake mine. He was enormous; a smoother, younger, more chiseled version of his dad. Paul Bunyan in his prime. I liked him instantly.

"You dating my sister?" he asked.

"Brian," Maggie scolded playfully as I feebly replied, "We're just friends."

"Can we get you a beer?" Mr. Stuard asked then barked, "Charlene, we need two beers in here," before I could respond.

Charlene arrived in seconds bearing the icy beverages and cooed, "Hey there, kiddo," with impossible enthusiasm. Now it was Maggie's turn not to stand. Her failure to fully acknowledge the lanky woman propelled a wave of tension through the room. "Who's this?" Charlene asked with forced playfulness. She turned her gaze from me to Maggie and said,

"I didn't know you were bringing a friend, Mag. I'll have to set another plate."

"This is Dan, hon," Mr. Stuard said.

"Hi, Dan. I hope you like meat. You're not one of them vegetarians are you?" she asked, then speed-walked from the room.

Mr. Stuard continued his verbal assaults on the entire officiating crew as Maggie and Brian shared quiet, mumbled, laughing conversation. As the first half ended Charlene called us all in to eat.

Maggie's grandmother sat next to me at dinner, materializing out of thin air or so it seemed. She reeked of cigarette smoke and was wide-eyed and fidgety. Based on Maggie's patient good humor, I gathered Grandma Stuard's grip on reality was loosening.

"You know, I was on the Mayflower," the old woman said to me as I spooned a portion of mashed potatoes onto my plate.

"You couldn't have been on the Mayflower grandma," Maggie interjected. "You weren't alive."

"Oh but I was," the old lady insisted. "The accommodations were quite lovely."

"How's the Impala running, Mag?" asked Brian.

"So far, so good. That gas gauge is still sticking."

"Well, let me know if anything else acts up. She can be a bitch sometimes."

The meal went smoothly. Maggie's dad, a High School football coach, recalled in vivid detail his teams disappointing playoff loss the weekend before. Brian, whose landscaping business survived the off-season by transforming into a snow-removal operation, bemoaned the tardiness of winter. Deanna provided us with a list of all the vegetables that gave her gas.

"I've been to the moon," Grandma Stuard confided to me

as our plates were cleared. "Back when they first started let-ting people go there."

"What was it like?" I asked.

"It was like walking on any other planet," she explained matter-of-factly.

Charlene lit the candles and we all sang happy birthday to Deanna. Maggie kept kicking my shin beneath the table. We forced down the rich chocolate cake and bid our good-byes in the kitchen doorway. Maggie couldn't get away soon enough.

Twenty minutes in to the drive home, she said, "I hope that wasn't too traumatic for you."

"They're not that bad, Maggie. No family's perfect."

"I know," she agreed. "I wish you could have met my mom, though, Fin. You would have liked her. Everybody liked my mom. There was just something special about her. She was the one everyone went to for help. If a kid fell and got hurt, he'd yell for my mom not his. That was just the thing you did in our neighborhood."

"I saw her pictures on the wall," I said. "You look just like her."

"I wish I could act just like her," she replied. "I need to be more patient with my dad and Charlene. It's not their fault they're dopey."

"How old were you when your mom died?" I asked.

"I was a junior in High School," she said. "Just like Ran-som."

Ransom. That was the longest we'd gone without saying his name. I was about to comment when the car began con-vulsing then sputtered to a stop.

"Oh shit," she said, coasting off to the side of the inter-state. "Shit, shit, shit!" She turned off the car and tried unsuc-cessfully to restart it. "We're out of gas. I can't believe it. We're out of fucking gas. I'm so sorry, Fin. I really thought we could make it to Pembrook. Did you happen to notice where the next exit is?"

"A mile and a half," I said. "I just saw a sign."

"That's not so bad."

It was a beautiful, crisp night. The moon was full and bright above the distant tree line. Occasionally a car would fly by and interrupt the cool tranquillity, but for the most part, we made our walk in peace.

"Can I tell you something, Finbar?" she asked shortly after we set out.

"Sure," I said, my heart suddenly pounding.

She waited to begin. My ears pulsed, temporarily deafened by the ocean of my blood.

"You know how I said Ransom spent the night with me last year?"

"Yeah."

"That was the night I lost my virginity."

I had no response. My first thought was an embarrassed and selfish one about the fact that I had yet to lose mine.

"It was a big deal to me, Fin," she continued. "A really big deal. And he seemed really different that night and the next day. Brighter. Happier. I was pretty crushed when he didn't write back over the summer. I'm kind of terrified of how he's going to write about it. Remember how blunt he was about that girl, Lizabeth? What if he talks like that about me?"

"I doubt he will, Maggie. If you want, you can read ahead to see what he says."

"That's okay," she said after considering my proposal. "I just wanted to mention it. I feel better now."

As we approached the exit sign I said, "Can I tell you something?"

"Anything," she answered.

"I can't remember one thing about finding Ransom in

his room that day. I completely black out on it. That's why I didn't know about that poem. I can't remember. I can't remember a thing. I don't know why I've been acting like I could."

"It's okay, Fin," she reassured gently. "I just figured it was too painful for you to talk about. Don't worry about it, all right?"

She took my hand and kept it all the way to the gas station.

January 17

Charlotte, my first and only girlfriend in the conventional sense, my 10th grade sweetheart. Charlotte would wait for me by the flag pole outside the high school and I'd walk her home. Charlotte and I would make out on the couch in her family room. I'd feel her small breasts through the material of her sweaters and turtlenecks. We'd French kiss the real way, our tongues extended, intertwining outside of our mouths. Then one day I saw Charlotte talking with Jake, the star of the football team, the brightest star in the firmament. They talked like old friends, they whispered, they leaned into each other. They hid their faces behind an open locker door. I saw them kiss, her hand resting on his abdomen. Hurt and relief co-mingled, overshadowed by healthy disdain. Hey Charlotte, I saw you with Jake, bummer about your lack of character. She was my last girlfriend, in the conventional sense.

She hadn't written a poem in years. She'd talk about it sometimes, but it became this mountain she just couldn't climb, or even face.

February 10

Today I met a girl named Maggie, my first conversation with a female since Lizabeth. Questions and smiles as we walked in the sunlight, questions and smiles from the girl with the faint trace of lavender on her lips. What do you see in me, Maggie? Why did you follow me after class and flutter your wings, your buttercup eyes, outside my No Trespassing sign? What would you possibly want with me, the invisible man, the Ghost of Harrison College, sad beyond belief? Please don't waste your time.

Maggie burst into tears, interrupting my reading. The sight of her name there in Ransom's rigid printing, the memory of his voice speaking it, overpowered her. I put my arm around her, and she nestled her head between my neck and shoulder, burrowing for comfort. I pulled her against the side of my chest and absorbed her sobs with my awkward, half embrace.

March 17
Her funeral looked like a glass menagerie: the casket, the trees, her friends from New York. We stood at her grave and listened to words she had written a decade before, as read by a tall man with a beard and ripped jeans. My dad held my hand and I let him, though I didn't feel anything, not for him, not for her, not for anyone. I milled about our crowded house then slipped away for silence. I returned to the river that held my soul and stared at the heartless sheen and listened for the language that long ago came to me, nature's child, imagination's choir boy. I listened for the language I spoke as a child, to no one, on endless summer afternoons. Silence all around. Silence within. Silence through the cold, black eternity. A secret burning gently in me. I walked home after dark, when I was certain they had gone.

Secrets. Crosses to bear.

April 17

Last summer. A slow Saturday afternoon. A hippie named Chaz saunters up as I sit on my standard sidewalk bench. I'd seen him before, a cross country cyclist, a dead head disciple, a rich dude from upstate America. He stands before me and he drills me with his sparkly hippie eyes and asks me if I've ever done shrooms. No, man, I haven't. Ah man you should. He lifts up his army green knapsack, unties it and sticks his hand inside. Out comes a clear plastic bag containing the harmless looking root. "It's on me," he says, and departs, whistling, laughing, the missionary pusher. I go for soup at Peter Christian's, the cream of asparagus I get every week. Behind my opened up weekly rag I break up the dry weed in the yellow green broth. I empty the bowl inside my belly. I hop on my bike and ride out of town to the swimming hole my mom and dad used to take me to on muggy Sundays. I sit and I wait for oblivion or enlightenment or whatever will come. The trees separate and divide around themselves. She rises from the water like a genie from a jar. She spins like an Olympic figure skater, so fast I can barely see her. Her hands hold an open book. Her poetry flies out like lightning rod grease flecks. They land on my skin. I stare at my blood flow. She opens her mouth and a maelstrom whirls within. The roar of water deafens me. She screams for me to reach for her. She pleads for explanations, wordless and loud, an angry deaf gypsy. I fall through the water glass. She disappears. I lay in a ball waiting for night to fall.

"Have you ever done anything like that, Finbar?" Maggie had the habit of asking whatever question popped into her mind. "Any drugs?" she clarified.

"Remember the night you came over to me outside the Nu Lamb party? Right after I punched the Okie from Muskogee in the face?"

"I remember," she said.

"That was my first time. I had a few hits of this guy's joint, which is why I was kind of quiet. I could hardly stand up."

Maggie laughed. "Are you kidding me? No wonder you were such a deadbeat."

"How about you?" I asked.

"There were about six months in high school where I got high all the time," she said. "I don't know what I was thinking. Then I just stopped. Haven't done it since. Isn't it crazy how Ransom's words flow so easily," she added. "It's like he's not even thinking and the words are just pouring out of him."

"Yeah," I agreed. "It's hard to believe that the person who wrote all this didn't know how to talk."

🍁

An Arctic blast hit that weekend, dissipating the remnants of summer. Actually, the temperature remained above freezing. It just felt like winter; epidermal atrophy. I left my class Saturday morning and walked into town, not admitting to myself what, or who, I hoped to find.

After putting it off for as long as my hatless ears could endure, I entered the Stonewall Book Store. The interior was deep and narrow, and a rack containing best-selling paperbacks stood three feet in front of the entrance, causing a traffic jam when three or more people arrived at the same time. Long wooden tables displaying new works of fiction stretched out behind it, their placement equally ill conceived.

To my delight, Maggie sat alone in the small cafe section at the back of the first floor. She wore jeans and a baggy sweater, and seemed engrossed by a massive textbook.

"Hi, Maggie," I said, startling her.

She smiled and pushed out a chair with her shoeless foot. Accepting her wordless invitation, I took off my coat and went to the counter for coffee. The first sips completed my body's warming process. I returned to the table and we settled into easy conversation. As I finished a second Danish, she leaned forward slightly.

"Let's go find Old John?" she said.

"Sounds good to me," I replied, relieved to be granted more time with her.

❦

The man in The Smoke Shop moved so slowly it almost seemed like he wasn't moving at all. His white hair was thick and uncombed. His face was perfectly blank. "Can I help you?" he asked in a tired, sandpaper voice when he finally reached the counter.

"We were wondering if you know where we could find a man named Old John," I said. "He knew a friend of ours and we need to talk with him."

"Old John," he repeated. "Old John lives in a room above the printers, that hippie couple, the Ithens. They rent it to him for next to nothing. He's been living there for years. What do you want with him?"

"We just want to ask him some questions," Maggie replied, "about our friend. They used to play chess together."

"That's Old John, all right. Best chess player in Pembrook. Says he won a big tournament in New York City back in the fifties. I believe him. He's hard to beat. I've only done it twice, and I've been playing him for twenty years. This time of day, you can probably find him in his apartment. He doesn't usually show his face until mid-afternoon on Saturdays. "Don't let him play you for money," he warned us as we turned to leave. "He'll rob you blind."

We walked two blocks down Main Street until we found the Ithens' shop.

"This must be it," Maggie said, pointing at the white door to the right of the store-front. I reached out and pressed the doorbell. A loud buzz echoed through the building. Moments later, we heard a muffled shout and the sound of heavy foot-steps. The door opened and Ransom's chess partner, Old John, squinted out at us. "What can I do for you?" he asked, not unkindly.

"We wanted to talk with you about a friend of ours, Ransom Seaborn."

His face lit up with recognition and his right hand emerged, holding a pipe, which he placed in his mouth. He was short and wide with a pasty complexion, and wore thick coke-bot-tle glasses through which his playful gray eyes sparkled.

"Ransom Seaborn, you say. Come on in." His voice was both lilting and raspy and implied a chuckle. We followed his Leprechaun frame and the sweet scent of his pipe smoke, up the steep staircase and into his one-room apartment. "Excuse the mess," he said, winded slightly from the climb. "It's been a long time since I had visitors."

I thought the place looked neat. Other than a few stains on the carpet, and the slightly unmade cot, which he indicated for us to sit on, things were in perfect order. He noticed me staring at the trophy on his nightstand.

"Won that in a chess tournament in New York City back in 1953. Only thing I ever won." He pulled a chair from the card table and placed it across from us. Before sitting down he said, "Can I get you anything? Wouldn't want to be rude now."

"No, thanks," we both replied. "My name's Dan Finbar," I continued as he took a seat.

"Maggie Stuard," Maggie followed.

"They call me Old John," he said. "Now what's this about Ransom? I thought he just got tired of beating an old man."

He hadn't heard.

"He beat you?" I asked without thinking.

"More often than I care to admit. I've never known anyone who could concentrate like him. Patience is the key to winning at chess, and Ransom has it."

Silence filled the room. Maggie and I looked at each other, unsure of what to say next.

"Ransom is dead, Old John," Maggie said finally. "He shot himself on September 21st."

I was grateful it was Maggie who'd told him.

"So he actually did it," he replied after a long pause, surprising us both. "I didn't want to think it, but I knew he had it in him."

This was plainly a man comfortable with death; who viewed death as a worthy adversary. His deeply creased face displayed curiosity, not grief.

"Some people consider themselves fixtures in this world," he elaborated. "Like me, for instance. I've always considered myself a fixture. Something that was going to be around, in the same place, day after day, for a long time. Something you could get used to. Ransom wasn't like that. He knew that his stay here was temporary. He carried that knowledge with him every minute of every day. Sitting with him in the park on the days we played chess was like sitting beside a shadow. It moves, and it moves, then it's gone with the darkness. I always had the feeling that Ransom was a shadow."

"Did he ever talk about killing himself?" Maggie asked.

"He didn't have to." Old John went on to tell us about the evening long ago when he'd sat alone, watching his father die in a hospital room. "I saw a light, plain as day, rise up from his body and float out the window. And I knew he'd passed," he said, smiling, ever smiling. "With our friend Ransom Seaborn, that light had already gone by the time I met him."

As we stood to leave, I had an inexplicable urge to hug this wise man. He kindly accepted my embrace and was delighted when Maggie followed suit.

"We'll see you again," I said at the door.

"The good Lord willing," he chuckled. "And if the creek don't rise."

Chapter Eight

Ryan got there first Monday night. I knew all their names by then: Wes, the thin, prematurely gray, Woody Allen sound-alike who rubbed his palms together anxiously when the Enterprise came under peril; Joel, the shy, socially awkward, brilliant one; Chuck, the revered malcontent, who showed up late, if at all; Mike, the tall, deep-voiced aristocrat; and Ryan, the soft-spoken cynic, who turned on the TV as I watched from our corner.

"Too loud?" he called over.

"No, it's fine," I answered, startled by the question. In the two weeks Maggie and I had been meeting there, we had never interacted with the *Star Trek* contingent.

"Space, the final frontier…"

I casually studied the room. Three love seats, soon to be occupied by the sci-fi viewers, surrounded a fake antique carpet. Chandeliers dangled above, hanging by thick chains, their electric Christmas candles ablaze. Wood beams cut across the high white ceiling, the trim to which bore imprints of the school logo—a flaming torch between a horse head and a dove. A square metal plate on the wall behind me read:

This dormitory is named by the
Trustees of Harrison College
In memory of Isaac C. Kessler
President of the college
From it's founding in 1876 until
His death in 1913

We were nearing the end of Ransom's sad musings. "We'll be done by Wednesday," I thought, as I heard the outer doors opening. Maggie entered, followed by Wes and Joel. Her cheeks were flushed from the cold. She looked beautiful.

"Sorry I'm late," she said. She took off her jacket and shoes and sat down. "Where are we?"

"The end of last semester," I answered.

"The big night's coming up," she said nervously.

"Sure you don't want to read ahead?"

"I'm sure. Let's just do it."

Her name began the first entry.

May 12

Maggie Stuard. You took me in and gave me hope when all hope had been wasted. You held me close, an angel in my fortress. Maggie, did I let you know how weightless I became? Was the deaf mute able to communicate just once, just this one time, in your arms and finally beyond his own dumb darkness? What will become of us, Maggie Stuard?

May 13

I watched you drive away in your brother's giant car. I felt a new kind of emptiness. The kind that includes the promise of fulfillment. I'll cling to this feeling all summer. I'll write it in words that I send you. I'll write it a hundred times.

September 1

It's either cop a whole new personality or plead the perpetual fifth. I choose the latter, again. What could I possibly have to say to these people, anyway? Yeah, Hanover. Yeah, English. Yeah, my mother died. Yeah, life fucking bums me out. Yeah, life doesn't make any fucking sense to me. Yeah, yeah, yeah.

There are no words to describe the last week of her life. Darkness. Candles. My father calling three times a day from Seattle. She's fine, I lied. She actually seems better. He'd be home Saturday. A day too late.

"What just happened, Fin?" Maggie asked. "Did we miss something?"

"I don't know. He seems to have reverted to his old self."

"Did we miss a page or something?"

"No, Maggie. Something must have happened over the summer."

"It must have happened early," she said. "I wrote him our first week home. God," she added. "That's so frustrating. I knew he was different. I knew he felt something."

"Isn't that kind of a good thing?" I suggested. "I mean... you were right. He changed. I know it was only for one page...but it's something."

"I guess," she replied. "It's almost harder though, Fin– knowing we were right on the brink of something. Knowing it was real, we were both on the same page, then having it go away before it even starts. It might almost be better for that night not to have happened. I mean it really crushed me over the summer when he didn't write back. Then it crushed me again when he pretty much ignored me this year. And then he crushed me one last time when he left us like that. That's a lot of crushing to endure. Does that make any sense?"

"Yeah, but in the long run I think you'll be glad to have had that time with someone you were drawn to so powerfully. And eventually your gratitude will outweigh your regret. Does that make sense?"

She smiled. "You're pretty good, Fin. Yeah. That does make sense."

❦

Matt was up when I got in that night, a rarity.

"What's going on, Mad Dog?" I asked.

"Chem test," he answered, looking up from his notebook, turning to grant me a brief interview. "Where were you?" My strange behavioral patterns had ceased to hold interest for him. He was making small talk.

"Taking a walk. Pembrook is beautiful this time of year," I said sarcastically. "Have you ever been?"

"Did you know that the founders of Harrison initially wanted to build the school in Angora?" he asked. He was still good for one such gem a week.

"Well, I'll be darned. They initially wanted to build in Angora, you say," I reiterated playfully.

"My sister had a baby tonight."

I'd known she was pregnant and due any day with his first niece or nephew; big news in the Price family.

"Congratulations. Boy or girl?"

"Girl. Pamela Ann. Seven pounds, three ounces." Our brief discussion of the joys of unclehood concluded with Matt saying, "By the way, Phil and I are having a little get together here Friday night, it's my twenty-first birthday."

By 'little get together' he meant just the three of us, I was sure. I also knew that bringing alcohol onto campus and drinking it in our room, an expellable offense, would be his single rebellious act as a college student.

"I think I'm free. I'll have to check my schedule," I replied in my best pampered prep school kid voice.

"Well, we'll be here."

※

The following evening I made it to Block ten minutes before they stopped serving dinner. Maggie and Jessica sat together near the salad bar.

"Hey, Fin," Maggie said as I approached.

"Hi, Dan Finbar," Jessica added.

"We just sat down," Maggie explained. "Come back and eat with us."

I grabbed some food then anxiously returned to their table where I took a seat by Jessica. As we began talking a group of guys burst through the entrance doors. J.D. was in their ranks.

"I'll be right over, Mag," he yelled, rushing to the kitchen before close.

"Should I leave?" I asked.

"Of course not," Maggie replied. "Why should you leave?"

"Just stay calm, Finbar," Jessica joked. "We don't need any bloodshed here."

"Does J.D. know about the journal?" I asked, looking at Maggie.

"Yeah," she answered. "Just relax, Fin."

I was incapable of doing as she said. Feelings fought for prominence within me. On the one hand, I was thrilled by the awareness that this was, in fact, an awkward situation. But I was also more aware than ever of my station in the college hierarchy: lowly freshman. While I bore an intuitive resentment toward J.D., I also viewed him as my natural superior.

Jessica welcomed him cheerfully as he took his rightful place beside Maggie.

He returned her greeting with equal good nature. "I'm J.D.," he said to me, lifting a hand in my direction. He was handsome and confident. I hated him.

"This is Dan Finbar," Maggie replied on my behalf.

"I remember seeing you at that Nu Lamb party, Dan. Sorry about Sully. He can be a real fathead. And sorry about your friend," he added. "What was his name again?"

"Ransom Seaborn," Maggie said sternly, "You know his name, J.D."

"Ransom Seaborn," he repeated. "I guess I do know what his name is…or was, I should say. So what year are you, Dan?" he asked though I sensed, again, that he knew the answer. I looked to Maggie for my reply but she remained silent, a little red in the cheeks.

"I'm a freshman," I said. "And I have to get going." The customary Finbar retreat from all things awkward. "Nice to meet you, J.D. See you later, Maggie?" I asked, my only jab in the invisible sparring match.

"I'll be there with bells on," she replied.

September 5

I didn't make it to class this morning. I sat at the desk in my room listening to a song over and over, "Late For The Sky," drinking coffee 'till my hands shook. I stared out the window, following meaningless bodies until they vanished from view, into buildings, out of my sight. She touches me in dreams, touches my face and my rumpled hair. She comforts and beckons simultaneously. I wake up crying, embarrassed by my wet pillow, my wet pillowcase. In dreams she opens my chest with a rusty knife and massages my heart. In dreams she sings her poems to me. In dreams she is alive still.

September 9

The evening wind blows through me, fresh from a nearby mountain. Maggie stops by the bench expecting me to say the things she has every right to hear. Not understanding why we're not picking up where we left off. She leaves me be after a quick hello. I am poison, Maggie. You don't know how lucky you are to be losing me.

Feather haired Magpie
Magical wood sprite
Conscience of pearly white
Voice like a song
Teary eyed Magdeline
Gentle toothed magistrate
Sorry to hesitate
Now I am gone

"I'm officially pissed off," Maggie declared. "What is this shit? Talk about melodramatic. His mom was already dead, for God's sake. My mom was dead, too. What could have been so terrible about last summer?"

I held my tongue. For some reason, I wanted to defend him. I doubted very much that he was being melodramatic. Whatever happened, whatever he had seen or done, was very real to him, and he was tortured by it. I let the moment pass and continued my reading.

September 11

My concentration's shot. Old John, older than any one, older than I'll ever be, older than clouds and trees, why did you look at me that way when I made the wrong move? Why did you wait so long before going for the kill? Old John, kindly

Old John, Am I the Hal to your Falstaff, or is it the other way around? What lessons are you trying to teach me with your fathomless eyes?

Sometimes I can almost forget. Sometimes it almost goes away. The words I speak push the truth from my mind for a moment, but only for a moment. Sometimes I almost forget.

September 15

I see myself in Finbar. Finbar the innocent, Finbar the fair, Finbar the young struggler. I see the thin trace of the one I could have been, if things had gone differently. We are the same in so many ways, you and I. Salinger, Van, melancholy. You sang about David, gone, and I heard the strains of sadness that echo in my brain, in my silence. We rode the Pembrook back roads tonight, eluding the law, drinking our beers. You felt like the brother I never had, the brother my parents mourned invisibly. The brother she left in a clinic in Maine or a hospital in Boston, the younger brother I think she saw, still, sometimes, who I saw sitting on her tombstone, a baby sobbing soundlessly. Finbar, don't you feel it? Our sad, blue-eyed connection. Almost a friend, almost a friend, almost a friend.

"It was one of those perfect afternoons," I began, compelled, somehow, by the entry. "I was flying…happy. I couldn't wait to play Ransom the CD I'd just bought. I was turning the knob when the gun went off. It scared the hell out of me."

I paused as the words and the dream's images finally connected. Maggie waited patiently, her hand on my forearm.

"It didn't quite compute, Maggie. You know? I heard the explosion and it freaked me out and everything, but I thought… I don't know what I thought. 'Terrible things don't happen to me.' 'There must be some explanation.' I ran into his room still feeling protected. Still anxious to play him that disc." My breath came more quickly as I recalled the horrifying events of that day. "He was on his bed. His legs were still moving. His head was back against the wall...eyes wide open. I can see it now, Maggie. The bloody paper. His chin propped up on his chest—the barrel of the gun still buried in his mouth. There was blood everywhere, Maggie."

The volcano that had been dormant in the center of my chest finally erupted, the molten lava flooding upward, through my throat and face, gushing from my eyes in the form of tears.

"Oh God, Maggie. Why didn't I get there sooner? Why didn't I save him?" I was sobbing now. She took me by the shoulders and pulled me against her. "Why couldn't I save him?" I cried as she rocked me like a baby.

"Finbar," she said softly straight into my ear, "there was nothing you could do. He'd already made up his mind."

We sat side by side on the steps outside Lawford. I felt awkward in the wake of my unraveling.

"God, Finbar, why have you been carrying that around with you all this time?"

"I don't know, Maggie. It's strange because it's all I ever dream about. I mean, any time I sleep it's there, like a home movie or something: I see it all. Soon as I wake up, it's gone. But tonight, I don't know, it finally connected. Something in that journal entry, I don't think I knew how guilty I felt for not getting there in time. For not seeing how truly fucked up Ransom was. Man, it feels good finally talking about all this."

"Call me any time you need to talk about it, Fin. I mean it. Any time."

Was she setting up the guidelines for our post-journal existence—I could call her, but only if I needed to talk about Ransom? Or was she simply comforting a friend?

I took an imaginary bullet to my imaginary heart, a fusil-

lade under the imaginary moon. Curious, the simulated peace
I felt as the brain dead earth reached up to receive me. If it
weren't for this incessant breathing, all would be right with
the world.

September 16

I'm so tired I can barely hold my head up. Why is this secret so vocal now? So loud and persistent? The walls shake
and spin around me. The ceiling lowers when I close my
eyes. How did I come to this hazardous pool? Why would life
lead me to darkness so early, a baby, still so new to light?
Heartless, illogical LIFE, bastard giver, bastard taker away.
A pale skinned baby I can't even kick or gasp or swim to the
surface for one last breath.

September 17

I wish I could hold my father in my arms, but that my arms
could grow longer and stronger first, that he might feel my
vast, unspoken love. I wish I could paint the sky's wan beauty
on a pad, and lift it from my pocket in the middle of the night.
I wish I could speak, just once, like I imagine everybody
speaking, knowing what they feel, turning it to pliable, reli-
able words that their listeners understand and take comfort
from. I wish I could sing at the front of the church, a timeless
gospel standard that would make the place weep and shake
with the power. I wish I could lift my heart to heaven, tearing
up my weakened roots and flying with the birds and the angels, flying with the pollen on the wind, landing on the cloud
of no regrets. I wish I could accept Finbar for my lonely, Harrison brother, a fraternity of sad seekers of blue eyed sunsets
and beauty sublime. I wish I could kiss Maggie hard on the
lips with an honest heart and clear eyes dancing. Of all the
girls I have ever known, you came the closest, Maggie. You
offered me redemption that night I don't talk about. You were

ready to come through for me but you were too good. But you were the closest, and this is the testament you'll never hear.

Maggie cried. I was jealous of Ransom at that moment. How did someone so reluctant to open up, so terminally backward in his relationship with the outside world, capture so precious a heart? Tentatively, I rested my hand upon hers. We were nearing the end, and we knew it. Just a few more minutes, a few more entries.

"Jesus, Finbar, I feel like all I ever do is cry. How do you put up with me?" The question was hypothetical. I would have answered gladly, possibly in song. "Why did he think he was no good? What made him decide he was unworthy of love? We're all worthy of love."

It was the angel in her talking.

"He just felt too much, same as his mother," I said, "and he missed her."

September 18
This campus is a dead end street, and I'm the dead end. Every one's asleep and I sit alone against the grain covering my tracks, blowing back over them with breath from my yellow lungs. No one can follow me here to this place with the quiet stillness all around. No one can follow me here. For the thousandth time, who the fuck are you, Ransom Seaborn? He has his mother's eyes and his father's ears. His mother's mind, and his father's heart. His mother's voice, and his father's hollow legs. His mother's cold, clammy, trembling hands.

September 19
Finbar asked, Do you believe in God? What did I say? Who cares or some such fucked-up posturing. Finbar, I'd

say if I could, of course I believe in God. I believe with the heart of a disgraced monk, who traded his vows for one night a week with the village whore. I believe like Judas in the aftermath. I believe like anyone who's ever tried and failed, who's ever come and gone.

Of all life's invisible comforts, the wind, by far, is the greatest one to me. I stand like a loosely hanging leaf and dare it to blow me away.

September 20

Haven't slept since Monday. Haven't even laid down. I hear voices when I close my eyes, her voices. The voices of all her life's moments, the voices of all her days and nights. The strong loud crying voice of her new-born self, the sing-song, jump rope voice of her summer day six year self, the breaking down voice of her twenty fifth birthday depression self, the clear, proud, sweet, rich, resonant voice of her highest, best poetry self, the screaming down tumbling voice of her dying night self. I hear them all, a dissonant symphony cued by my eyelids' obstruction of my eyes, reacting to each wave of my arms. Me, the mad conductor. I'm turning into her. I know it more with each passing moment. I feel it more with each labored intake of breath. It is my clearest awareness. It is my destiny. She's struggling, still, to find her voice, only through me now.

We stared silently at the space where the missing last page had been, unsure of what to say or do next.

"What do you think he did with it, Finbar?"

"I have no idea."

It felt like summer camp ending, summer camp in which we had endured some hardship and lived to tell the tale. But this was a summer we wouldn't relive by warm memories. No one would understand. We stood on the sidewalk outside her dorm and I gathered up my courage.

"I was wondering if you'd want to do something Friday," I blurted. "Maybe see a movie."

Screw Matt's party. I couldn't accept the thought of not being with her again, and soon.

"I'm supposed to go to some dance with J.D., Fin."

"No problem," I said, trying to sound unaffected.

"Some other time, though," she added, forcing my eyes to stay with hers. "I have to tell you, Fin, as painful as it's been, I've loved reading this journal with you. I know there are still some questions that we'll probably never know the answer to, but I think it really helped to bring some closure for me."

"Me, too."

"What I'm trying to say is thank you. You were the perfect person to share this loss with. Does that sound crazy?"

Suddenly I was fighting tears. I couldn't speak. She started crying herself then.

"Thanks, Finbar," she repeated, then pulled me into a forceful embrace before running for her dorm.

"Good-bye, Maggie," I whispered to no one.

❧

Later that night, I lay awake contemplating the sadness I felt. I was saying goodbye, for good now, to the sad stranger who had become a part of me, who had illustrated for me, in shocking, vivid detail, life's brutal impermanence. And already I ached for Maggie's company as I reveled in my chance, bonus discovery: romantic love, albeit unrequited.

The weather's turning. The two times I left the room today it's been at least ten degrees colder. The heater isn't working so I put on my coat late this afternoon. It's almost midnight now. December 23rd. Freezing rain pelts the window.

I have never been further from understanding the meaning of this life. Time passes. Decisions are made. Destruction and cruelty appear where no such things were expected, yet beauty and generosity abound. The human spirit triumphs and falters in fast-moving cycles. Nothing makes sense.

Earlier this evening I happened to glimpse my reflection in the mirror. With the lost weight and the facial hair—and the trusty cigarette, of course—I look just like him. I remember the feeling I had shortly after he died that I was turning into him, becoming him. Before too long here we can measure the merit of my prophecy.

Chapter Nine

If Phil Fercheck had got his way, the volume would have been much louder. He insisted we huddle around the tiny speakers while he directed our attention to the high points of *One of These Nights,* the featured Eagles song of our third hour.

"Do you hear that bass line?" he asked. "Amazing bass player—Randy Meisner. He'll be replaced by Timothy B. Schmidt. I can't decide who is more amazing."

"So the Eagles are pretty much amazing then, Phil," I replied flatly, not that he could hear me through his rapture.

"Shh," Matt said for at least the twelfth time. "Did you hear something?"

"I think its campus security, Matt. They have the place surrounded," I answered. "Better start packing your things."

He didn't laugh. Though he had purchased a fifth of rum and successfully smuggled it into the building, a life of crime did not agree with him. The more he drank, the more paranoid he became.

Unable to contain himself any longer, Phil bellowed along with the record at three times its volume.

"Shut the fuck up, Phil," Matt pleaded, sounding like

a foreign exchange student, maybe from Japan, new to the world of American slang.

"Matt, will you lighten up? Jeez oh man," Phil pouted, but followed the birthday boy's request.

"So how's it feel, Mad Dog? Do you feel older?" I asked — trying to initiate a non-Eagles-based conversation. I refilled my empty glass, one part Coke, three parts rum.

"It felt kind of cool getting served in the liquor store," he said. "I kept thinking they'd turn me down or kick me out or something. I felt older then, I guess. It's no big deal, though."

"No big deal?" Phil asked, horrified. "No big deal? Of course it is. Now you can go to any bar in the country and meet women. As of this day, your horizon is infinitely broader, no pun intended."

The corners of Phil's mouth were dotted with thick white pockets of spittle. He reminded me a little of Goofy, the Disney character. Of my two drinking buddies, he was definitely the more delusional. At least Matt knew he'd never pick up a girl in a bar. Phil saw such things as imminent.

I shut out the music and the conversation and focused my thoughts on Maggie. I wondered if I'd even crossed her mind since we parted ways two days before. I wondered what she was doing, what she was wearing, if she was having a good time.

"Finbar," Matt said, "Finbar, I'm talking to you."

"Sorry, I must have spaced off there." I felt light headed. My body was warm.

"Do you want to go in on a pizza?"

"Sure," I said, suddenly famished, suddenly drunker than I thought I was. I didn't know how much I'd had, but the bottle was nearly empty and my cohorts seemed curiously sober.

Phil left to get a coupon from his room (ever the bargain

shopper) and place the order. The instant we had the room to ourselves I said, "I think I'm in love, Mad Dog."

"With who?" he asked, disbelief in his frail soprano.

"I'm not at liberty to say," I replied as Phil tapped on the door that Matt had locked the instant he left. "Let's just say she's somewhat problematic."

"I know who it is," Matt said, standing and crossing the room.

"Thirty minutes or less," Phil reported upon re-entry. "If not, we don't have to pay. What time is it exactly?"

"Eleven thirty," Matt replied. "It's that girl you went to Erie with that night isn't it?"

"Exactly?" Phil repeated, dubious. "Who's the girl he went to Erie with?"

"Eleven thirty," I blurted. "Did you say eleven thirty?" I stood abruptly, looking at my naked wrist. "I'm late for a very important appointment," I declared in my best Jimmy Stewart *It's a Wonderful Life* voice. "I have to go."

"What the hell," Matt said as I grabbed my coat and darted from the room.

The alcohol hit me harder with the swift and sudden motion. I tumbled down the last four steps and fell to the floor at their base. Rising to my feet, I leaned and opened the heavy West Terrace door.

🍁

I posted my vigil on a stone bench in the courtyard outside of Maggie's dorm that offered a clear view of the illuminated doorway. When she came in, if she came in, I would definitely see her. Heavy, wet flakes, the season's first snowfall, fell from the sky.

Jessica Newman passed by en route to the entrance.

Though I could count on one hand the conversations we'd had, our bond transcended mere conversation.

"Jessica, over here!" I shouted.

"Finbar? Is that you?"

She walked over and sat beside me. It occurred to me then that I didn't really have anything to say without spilling my guts all over the place.

"Someone's been drinking," she said without malice. "Where were you?"

"My roommate turned twenty-one today. We celebrated in our room. I drank a little bit." She laughed at the understatement and my noble attempt to appear sober. "What's so funny?"

"You're so funny. What are you doing here?"

"Enjoying the fine November night," I said.

"This wouldn't have anything to do with my roommate, would it?"

"Of course not. I just have a fondness for this bench. It's very firm." After a short pause, in which my right elbow slid off of my right knee twice, I added, "Tell me something interesting about yourself, Jessica." Even I knew I was slurring.

"Okay," she replied as she stood to leave, "I don't like talking to people when they're wasted. No offense."

"I wouldn't say I'm wasted. I'm not a hundred percent sober, but I wouldn't say I'm wasted."

"Well, Finbar, whatever you are, try not to do anything you'll regret."

"It's not quite that simple," I said, five minutes after she'd gone.

❧

Maggie and J.D. date arrived an hour later. I'd been periodically checking the lobby wall clock through the window.

In that time, I had urinated twice on the trunk of a nearby poplar tree, written and rehearsed several eloquent speeches, thought that I might be sick, and repeatedly cursed the fact that I didn't own gloves or a hat. I stared intently as she leaned into her date, and kissed him on the lips. Or was it the cheek? Luckily, she waited as he walked away. Otherwise, I might have been locked outside in the cold.

"Maggie," I whispered, not ten feet away. "Maggie, it's Fin."

"Finbar, what are you doing here?"

The million-dollar question.

—"What is anybody really doing here?"

—"I drew first watch, quiet so far."

—"I'm madly in love with you and wanted to make sure your date didn't mistreat you."

All viable answers, but I opted for none of the above. Instead I surprised her, turning the tables with, "What are you doing here? I mean, how was your date?"

"Do you mean my date as a person, or my date as an event?" She was trying to lighten the situation, act buddy-buddy with me.

"Don't get cute," I said, turning sharper than I'd meant to, feeling a particular form of anger, irrational and fluid, that I would later come to associate with hard liquor. "What's your problem?" I asked, surprising her again. I was on a roll.

"What do you mean what's my problem? What's your problem?" Her voice rose in irritation, just above speaking, not yet a yell.

"Ransom was still warm in his grave and you were painting the town with old J.D." I had never used that phrase before, 'painting the town.' It didn't feel right. It reminded me of Matt's cuss attempts. "What the fuck, Maggie?" Speaking of cussing, I was gathering dangerous momentum. She started to respond, but I ignored her, continuing my rant. "I thought you loved him, Maggie. I thought he meant something to you. How could you forget about him so quickly?"

Any psychiatrist worth his salt would have known to substitute 'me' for 'him,' 'I' for 'he.'

"Maggie Stuard is a no good whore!" I screamed through my trusty hand megaphone, Bart Starr shouting audibles to his wide-outs on the frozen tundra of Lambeau Field. I imagined countless Harrison virgins stirring from their peaceful sleep, picking up a disturbance on their Christian bliss radars. "Maggie Stuard is a no good whore!" I cried again. It would have been funny if it weren't so outrageous. What was I doing? I cared more for Maggie than for anyone in the world at that moment. Why was I tearing her down? Why was I accusing her of things I knew to be untrue? Why? Why? Why?

"Finbar," she tried again more gently, realizing, perhaps, how drunk I was.

"No, Maggie," I pleaded, "don't say a word. You'll only make it worse." I waved my arm emphatically. "I have to go. I don't think we should see each other any more," I added, ignoring the fact that we probably weren't going to anyway. "You didn't care about Ransom anyway. Who the hell are you kidding?"

She stood in silence as I walked away.

❧

Before it was over, I would get belligerent with a cashier at the Podunk, search half-heartedly for my nemesis Okie, and donate my dinner to the Weir C. Kessler memorial garden. For good measure, on returning to my floor, I searched through my wallet for Lisa Starzel's phone number. I'd placed it there that summer in the hopes that I'd be asking her out one day. Her father answered on the third ring.

"Yeah," he muttered through layers of sleep.

Summoning all of my strength and determination I said as clearly as was humanly possible, "I Need. To Speak. With Lisa. Please." I reminded myself of Audrey Hepburn in *My Fair Lady.*

"Who is this?"

"Harry Houdini."

"Lisa's asleep!"

The line went dead.

❦

I slept through my class Saturday, or, rather, stayed passed out. When I finally arose in the early afternoon, I felt like someone had dumped a bottle of Elmer's glue down my throat, all dried up and pasty. I spent the day as a shut-in, not venturing from the confines of my hall for fear I might encounter Maggie or someone else I had offended the night before.

"Maggie Stuard is a no-good whore!" I almost cried remembering the words. With hangover logic I forced myself to believe it was better this way. Maggie and I didn't have anything in common. She was too old, I was too young, and Ransom's presence was too intrusive. The situation could only cause me pain. And though the split had been ugly and spontaneous, it was for the best. Who needed women anyway? Maybe I'd join a monastery.

❦

Late that night, after two pizza deliveries and twenty-five pages of *A Passage to India,* I ventured to the laundry room in the basement of Kessler. Though Thanksgiving break was just days away, my underwear was heading into its thirty-sixth hour.

The clean, steamy heat put off by the dryers quickly re-

placed the November chill. The room was bright and spare.
A chrome and enamel table stood in the middle, between the
opposing lines of washers and dryers, for folding.

Though it was nearing midnight, I wasn't alone. A balding,
bearded sophomore pushed the last of his wet clothes into the
far dryer, stuck in two quarters and pressed the start button.
Then he sat atop the machine and leafed through his paper-
back textbook. He wore a tie-dyed t-shirt with the Grateful
Dead insignia on the left breast pocket. I set the water to hot
and threw in a capful of detergent.

"Mabry?" he asked, noticing my novel.

"Yeah," I replied, startled by the sound of his voice over
the whirring machinery.

"Freshman English?"

"Yeah."

"I took that last year. Is that your third book?"

Together we reviewed the course syllabus and compared
notes on our likes and dislikes. The edges of his mouth turned
upward regardless of what he did or said. He looked like The
Joker on valium. A kinder, gentler arch-villain.

"What are you reading?" I asked.

"It's called *The Buddha in Daily Life,*" he answered, with
what I later learned was a Buffalo, NY accent. "I got it in the
mail today. A friend of mine sent it. I was just reading about
the Ten States of Life." He looked down to an opened page
and recited, "'Hell, Hunger, Animality, Anger, Tranquillity,
Rapture, Learning, Realization, Bodhisattva and Buddha-
hood.' We're all in one of these states at every moment," he
added, paraphrasing.

"I think I'm stuck in hell," I said to myself as much as to
him, remembering again my drunken antics. "You better not
let anyone see you with that," I added. "They might send you
to prison or something."

By the time he'd retrieved his dry laundry, I'd discovered

his name—James—his main hobby, playing drums. His passion, The Grateful Dead. As he was leaving, I asked if he'd ever seen them play.

"Does Rose Kennedy have a black dress?" he replied.

❧

By Monday afternoon, I'd hit the wall. Classes that morning were spent in a fog. I didn't look up when walking between buildings. I returned to my room the instant Creative Writing concluded, more depressed than ever.

When Matt got back from lunch I asked, "Do you think Phil would loan me his car for a few hours. I need to get out of here. Want to go to the Landmark or something?"

"You're under age," he replied, not bragging, merely stating a fact. Seeing my look of indifference he continued, "I have a Chem lab. Phil's in Mellon, 117. He'd probably loan it to you."

"See you later," I said.

"Don't get drunk," he yelled after me as I went down the stairs.

❧

I nursed my first beer, a 16-ounce bottle of Budweiser. Phil had been surprisingly generous with his car, probably because I told him I needed to get to the record store in Angora to pick up *Hotel California.*

"Leave it where you found it," he said, handing me his keys with a smile. "Enjoy."

The bartender had also been surprisingly generous, not questioning my age or lack thereof. I think he was glad for the company. I was the only one in the place.

"This is my favorite show," he said, pointing to the TV suspended in the upper right hand corner, "People's Court." A guy was accusing his former girlfriend of mistreating the pet parakeet they had purchased together. He wanted custody. Of course, the bird was in the courtroom with them, staring eagerly at the wise, old judge. "Damn right boy, you tell her," yelled the short, spry barkeep, who'd introduced himself as Pete.

Hank Williams Jr. sang softly from a jukebox in the background, complaining of a tear in his beer. The buxom St. Pauli girl smiled from her paper rectangle above the two rows of bottled liquor. The walls were lined with animal heads and road signs, along with the random musical instrument. I felt instantly at home.

It was close to seven when Maggie walked in. I was in the middle of my second beer. Only one other customer had arrived since I'd been there, an older gentleman who sat four stools down complaining about gas prices. Maggie took the stool to my left.

"Coors Lite," she said to Pete, who had the bottle opened and in front of her in seconds.

"How'd you find me?" I asked.

"Your roommate said you might be here. You're not drunk are you?"

Translation: you're not going to act like an asshole again, are you?

"No," I replied, to both questions. I looked up at the TV screen, local news.

"How'd you feel Saturday morning?" she asked.

"Like I'd been forced through a cement mixer. I didn't make it to class."

"What were you drinking?"

"Rum." The forecast called for snow. A cloud poured flakes behind the meteorologist's head. "I'm sorry for the way

I acted Maggie, and for what I said. I didn't mean one word of it."

She placed her hand over mine and said, "Let's get out of here."

❧

The green outline of a leaf illuminated the sign in the empty parking lot of the Cloverleaf Motel. The vacancy light flashed on and off beneath it. Neither of us had spoken a word during the five-minute ride.

"Wait here," she said, putting the Impala in park outside the office. We'd left Phil's car at the Landmark.

I listened to the hum of the engine, felt my uneven breaths quickening and catching, and did not allow myself to think about what was happening. A light snow fell gently on the windshield, melting on contact.

"Room 29," she said, holding a key, and pulled the car across the parking lot. Inside, we removed our jackets and threw them onto the badly nicked wooden dresser. We sat on the edge of the lone double bed. The table lamp cast a small ring of light, our candle for the moment. The only sounds were our breathing and the wind outside the window.

"I've been thinking about you all weekend, Finbar. I almost called you about twenty times, but I didn't want to let you off the hook so easy. You were a real jerk on Friday."

Though most of me was concentrating on her every word, there was that small part, that eighteen-year-old-driven-by-hormones part, that couldn't help reflecting on the fact that I was alone in a motel room with a beautiful woman.

"I know, Maggie," I replied. "I don't know what I was doing. I think I was just afraid of not seeing you any more."

"You have a strange way of showing it." She laughed, then smiled. "By the way, just before your little tirade I called it off with old J.D. We never really clicked anyway." She paused, moving closer. "How are you doing?" she asked, smiling half-way.

"I'm a little nervous," I said.

"Me, too."

She leaned toward me and our lips touched for the first time. My heart was a factory-fresh trampoline, my mind a flood of sensation. She guided me backwards. We lay on the still-made bed, our legs bent over the bottom edge. We moved our bodies fitfully, holding and pulling and clutching at hair. Our tongues danced free-form together, long lost lovers, faithful all this time. I reached my hand under her cotton sweatshirt and felt her bra's exterior like a blind man reading Braille. She found the hard metal of my belt buckle, her fingers brimming with promise.

My hard-on strained against my jeans, a separate creature, though closely allied with its master. Allied until, long before the appropriate moment, it erupted like Vesuvius, soiling my underwear, breaking my resolve. I turned away, panicked and ashamed.

"Finbar," she whispered, "what's wrong?"

"Nothing," I lied. The six-year old that just wet the bed.

"Finbar, tell me what's wrong."

"I just made a mess of myself," I stammered. "I came, Maggie." A simple, yet painful admission.

She smiled and then stood. Methodically, she untied my shoes and pulled them from my feet, removing the socks as well. She unbuckled my belt and pulled off my jeans. She removed my soggy briefs and threw them in the wastebasket, symbolically demonstrating that the awkward moment had passed. Without a word, she walked to the sink and wet a towel with warm water. Returning to the bedside, she leaned down and rubbed the damp cloth on my belly, before sponging a downward trail. The resurrection was complete by the time she'd taken off her sweatshirt, bra, socks, jeans, and panties and climbed on top of me.

Later, we lay in the darkness and I held her close. Her head rested on my chest.

"So what'd you think?" I asked, giddy. "I mean, other than the first part, was I all right?"

"Not bad," she said. "Needs some work though."

"Are you kidding? I was masterful."

"Yes, you were slightly masterful. You're a natural."

We laughed until tears filled our eyes. It was the happiest I'd been in my entire life.

I kissed her on the forehead and said, "I love you, Maggie." The words were out before I could even consider their implication.

"I love you too, Finbar."

She fell asleep in my arms.

❧

The God I had ignored since the day of Ransom's death, the God who had betrayed me and turned a blind eye on my tortured friend was with me then, as real to me as Maggie was. He was the ceiling above our heads that I couldn't see in the unfamiliar darkness. He was the musky odor of last week's cigarette smoke that permeated the cheap room. He was the hope that sprang to life in me as she ministered to my emptiness and my longing for love and affection. He was her skin, her eyes, and her willingness to receive me in all of my ragged confusion and tender uncertainty.

"Thank you God for bringing her to me," I whispered, almost silently. "Thank you God for this life which I so often take for granted. Please be with us as we struggle to understand ourselves. Please be with Ransom, wherever he is, and guide him into the never-ending light of your mercy. Amen."

I slept soundly for the first time in two months.

※

The strangeness of my surroundings awakened me before dawn, my subconscious asking, 'Where the hell are we?' The prayer on my lips as I'd drifted to sleep had settled in my heart through the night. I turned onto my side and stared at her back, which moved with the soft rhythm of her breathing. I rested my hand on her side, reassuring myself that she was really there, that she was not an apparition.

My mind ran freely from thought to thought, gradually moving toward a realization: I had no right to hold on to Ransom's journal. It belonged to his father. Furthermore, I'd take it there myself. Hanover, New Hampshire held the answers to our questions. That was where I had to go.

Maggie stirred and awakened beside me. She rolled over, smiled, leaned in and kissed me on the cheek. I informed her of my decision, explaining as well as I could my desire to see where Ransom lived, to speak with his dad, to deliver his journal in person and put this all behind me.

"Can I go with you?"

"I think I need to do it alone, Maggie," I replied. "Besides, one of us will be enough for Mr. Seaborn to handle. I promise I'll tell you every single thing that happens."

"Do you still respect me?" she asked.

"Does Rose Kennedy have a black dress?" I'd been waiting to use that line. It got a chuckle from Maggie.

"Seriously, Fin, do you think this was a mistake?"

"What?" I asked, feigning amnesia. "Who are you anyway? What are we doing here?"

"So you're all right with what happened last night?"

"I've never been better, Maggie."

For an exclamation point I pulled her toward me, her naked breasts pressing against my chest, my fingers dancing along the small of her back, beneath the cover of her flowing brown hair.

❧

"Mr. Seaborn," I said that evening into the phone at the end of my hall, "my name's Dan Finbar. I was a friend of your son's."

So began the awkward conversation in which I invited myself to Joel Seaborn's home that Friday, the day after Thanksgiving. This after calls to my father, Greyhound and New Hampshire Information.

"Sure, Dan," he said, "that would be no problem."

I hesitated.

"I found him that day, Mr. Seaborn. I'd been spending some time with him before then. I just wanted to talk to you about it." I didn't mention the journal.

From Ransom's account, I had gathered that this was a man accustomed to talking things through, who was open to sudden turns in the road. I pictured him as I saw him outside Ransom's room, red-eyed and broken. I felt a strange affinity for him at that moment, like I was his son once removed.

"The only bus gets in to White River Junction at midnight." I explained. "Do you think you could pick me up? I know it's a pain."

"I'll be there," he said, sounding cheerful, almost.

❧

"The great equalizer," I said, commenting on the snow, which had just gotten heavier. "It makes even ugly things beautiful."

Maggie and I had been walking for less than an hour.

We'd met at midnight, by the bench in front of Rockwell, and followed the sidewalk wherever it led. The next morning we would travel to our respective homes for Thanksgiving break.

"That's how I think of God's mercy," I continued. "It's like snow falling on all of us, making even our ugliness beautiful. You could pick the sun or the wind, I guess, but I like the snow because it's so silent and peaceful, and it can turn into water."

She stopped us in our tracks and we kissed for at least five minutes in the middle of the deserted sidewalk. I thought I might crack a rib from the force of our embrace. I wouldn't have minded, really. It would be nice to have a steady reminder, even a painful one, of this perfect moment.

I was seized by a desire to describe to her, in minute detail, exactly what I felt right then: love, blossoming, a flower in my chest, light, flowing through my veins and eyes. I almost spoke, but opted instead just to look at her.

Chapter Ten

I stepped onto the Greyhound shortly before five, the morning after Thanksgiving. We'd pull into White River Junction by midnight—seventeen hours to pause and reflect.

Why was I doing this? I could easily have dropped the journal in the mail, along with a short note saying how much I'd liked Ransom and how sorry I was for Mr. Seaborn's loss. The development between Maggie and I had assured my return to the world of functioning people. Why this sidetrack? What did I hope to accomplish?

I decided that somewhere inside of me I had intended all along to make this trip: A pilgrimage to bring closure to an unexpected chapter in my life. I wanted to see Ransom's world, to give depth to this character that had dominated my thoughts for so long, and maybe then say good-bye to him, after I knew him better. Mostly, it was just a deep, instinctive feeling. I had to go to Hanover. I had to see his father again. That was the bottom line.

The trip turned grueling by the ninth hour. A young man in his early twenties had gotten on in Carlisle. He had some kind of mental condition and twitched and muttered all the way to Boston. Each time I drifted to sleep, his voice would rise slightly in private, psychotic exclamation.

Idly, my thoughts drifted to the day before, Thanksgiving. Mass that morning was different than the last time. I paid attention, prayed, and happily gave my parents and Sara the sign of peace. I thought of Maggie as I left the pew and walked up the center aisle for Communion. I smiled as the host melted on my tongue. "Only say the word and I shall be healed."

Our house was alive with activity. Ann and Bob were in from Akron with their two kids, Christine and Bobby, three and five. Their innocence filled us with awe and amusement. Kim and Tom arrived around three, just before John and his girlfriend, Rose. The grown-ups drank Cold Duck in the kitchen, the minors, soda in the dining room. We all stuffed ourselves with turkey and cranberry sauce as the gray, happy day turned to evening. I sensed that people were more comfortable around me then they'd been before. They spoke to me freely, their faces unclouded by looks of concern. My self-imposed exile had ended. I soaked in the laughter of the long-running jokes and felt reunited with my own flesh and blood.

At one point I smiled, imagining myself standing at the dinner table and saying, "This Thanksgiving I am most thankful for the fact that I lost my virginity. Would anyone care to join me in a toast?"

※

"White River Junction" the driver announced over the squeaking brakes. I stepped outside and walked into the dead, late-night bus station. Mr. Seaborn, the only non-employee in the place, greeted me with a smile.

"Hello, Dan," he said, extending his hand.

"Hi, Mr. Seaborn," I replied, following as he led the way to the parking lot.

"Please call me Joel, Dan."

"People call me Fin," I said. "Short for Finbar."

"Good Irish name. What's your father do, Fin?"

"He's principal of a grade school by our house. We all went there."

"How many's all?" he asked, opening the back door of his big, red Suburban and placing my bag on the seat.

"Five," I answered. "I had a brother who died when I was little, though."

I don't know why I included that information. It's not something I normally said.

"I'm sorry to hear that."

We slipped into easy conversation as we made the half-hour drive down 91. He had the uncanny ability to make you feel like he had known you all your life, like your comments and your thoughts were important to him, on a personal level. He filled me in on the family history.

"I met Ransom's mom at NYU a million years ago. God, she was beautiful. I loved her on sight." He smiled with the memory. "It took her a while to reciprocate, but eventually she got the idea.

"When we graduated, I got a job with the publishing house that put out her first collection of poetry. We got married in January of the following year. Ransom came along one year later.

"Ransom Seaborn," he continued. "What a name to give a little baby. No wonder he was so serious. If I'd only stopped drinking a little earlier I might have spared him such a weighty title. At the time, his mother and I thought it was perfect.

"Anyway, when Ransom was three we moved here from New York. Rosemary was getting kind of run down, and we didn't particularly care for the rat race. She wrote. I served as her agent. And I'd still work with certain authors my company was publishing. That was why I traveled so much. Still do.

"How did you meet Ransom?" he asked, briefly redirecting his gaze from the road to my outline in the darkness. "I didn't think he talked to anyone at Harrison."

"I was definitely the exception," I began, and told him the story of my first few weeks at Harrison. "I think the key was the fact that I loved Van Morrison. That seemed to go a long way with Ransom. The Salinger thing didn't hurt either."

"He loved to read, all right," he interjected, "ever since he was a little boy. I thought he would be a writer one day." After a long silence he said, "So you're into Van?"

By the time we stood in the living room of his single-story country home, it was after one o'clock. A fireplace sat opposite the brown leather sofa, which was flanked on either side by an end table and easy chair. A painting of a river hung above the mantle. Two framed poems adorned the wall that divided the living and dining rooms.

"I'm sure you're tired," he said. "I thought you could sleep in Ransom's room."

"Sounds good."

We walked down the hallway to the last door on the left.

"I might not be here when you wake up in the morning. Please make yourself at home. And I'm not just saying that, Fin."

As he walked away, I said, "Thanks, Joel, for letting me come here, and for being so kind."

"It's good to have some company," he replied. I hadn't considered the possibility that Joel might not want to be alone this holiday weekend, his first as his family's sole survivor. "Good night, Fin."

❧

Ransom's room was different than I thought it would be: warmer, more lived-in. I guess I expected another version of his dorm room. The big surprise was the photographs: a few of his mom and dad, and at least a dozen of outdoor scenes. Ransom had quite the eye.

His desk was neat and uncluttered but still held proof of his existence, his personality. Brick bookends held up a collection of his favorite novels: *The Catcher in the Rye, For Whom the Bell Tolls, The Grapes of Wrath.* A poem of his mother's called *Field Full of Heather* was displayed in a standing picture frame. A clock ticked loudly from beside a bent, spring-armed lamp, which I turned on and off.

I couldn't resist checking his drawers. In his journal, he'd implied that he'd never recorded his thoughts like that before, but I was curious. Maybe I'd find a stash of letters he'd written but not sent, or poems he'd been working on. No such luck. The top drawer held a collection of his mother's, the one Joel had mentioned in the car, and three empty spiral notebooks. A baseball rolled over a broken watch as I opened the middle drawer. The bottom drawer was empty.

I went to the bathroom and brushed my teeth. Returning, I changed into shorts and a t-shirt, killed the overhead light and climbed under the cool sheets. In spite of the strangeness of my situation, it wasn't long before I drifted to sleep.

I awakened hours later. The bedside clock read 3:15. My first thought was of *Amityville Horror*, a book I had read when I was too young, about a house possessed by demons. The main character was lured from his sleep every night at precisely 3:15. For weeks I would wake up and wait until I was sure that the moment had passed. And every night, the clock gave the same terrifying reading when finally I let myself look.

I recalled the journal entry Ransom had written about sneaking out of his room to swim in the river when he was a child. Feeling brave and restless, and nowhere near sleep, I decided to re-enact his ritual.

I dressed in the warmest clothes I'd packed, long underwear, jeans and a sweatshirt, and went to the hall closet and grabbed my coat. I returned to the room and climbed through the window, which I pulled down but not shut, behind me. The yard, the entire scene, looked much like I'd imagined from the journal, except for the light dusting of snow. I wished I had a cigarette as I followed the path he'd laid out, across the street—Haymaker was it?—and down the Limegrover's driveway. The sudden, frantic barking of a dog from inside the house sent me running through their back yard, nearly colliding with a stone structure of some sort.

On faith and faith alone I descended the dirt hill, feeling my way through the darkness. Blindly, I forced my way through the brittle-branched trees and snow-clumped thickets.

At the bottom, the moon off the water illuminated my surroundings with breathtaking effect. I understood instantly why Ransom had chosen this as his escape. The landscape, the tree-lined Connecticut River, embodied tranquility.

I also understood why Ransom had shifted out of first person in that entry. This place, those secret sojourns, represented an innocence he could no longer claim for his own. The thirteen year-old boy was gone forever.

I stood erect, breathing in the cool air as deep as my lungs would receive it; breathing in the memory of a sensitive child hiding from the world, hiding from his own impulses, hiding from the mother he loved and feared.

🍁

Joel kept his word. When I got out of bed at ten thirty the next morning, he was gone. I showered and entered the kitchen, opened the refrigerator, stared out the window. I decided to walk into town, a half-mile or so. I knew the way from the drive in the night before.

The main drag was quiet, the majority of the Dartmouth student body home for the holiday. All that remained were the natives. I explored my surroundings at a snail's pace, pausing to gaze into each new storefront: The Dartmouth Book Store, the Hanover Inn, Everything But Anchovies. Peter Christian's, the restaurant in which Ransom had taken mushrooms, jumped out at me from across the street. Looking both ways, I crossed and entered the quiet, Old English pub.

"How's it going?" a fortyish waitress with graying black hair asked as the door closed behind me.

"You open?"

"We're always open, and I'm always here, or so it seems." She smiled, not nearly as downhearted as her words might indicate. "What can I get for you?"

And so I experienced another Ransom landmark. For good measure, I ordered the cream of asparagus soup.

❧

Back at the house, Joel sat at the circular white kitchen table, sipping from an oversized mug.

"There's coffee on if you want it," he said, pointing to the counter-top contraption. "Cups are in the closet right in front of you."

I filled one and sat down across from him.

"How'd you sleep?" he asked politely.

"To be honest with you, I had some trouble. It felt strange being in Ransom's bed." After a sip of the bitter, dark brew, I stood and walked down the hallway to the room in which I'd slept, reached into my bag and pulled out the journal. I paused briefly to feel it's weight in my hands, to possess it, one last time. "This belongs to you," I said, placing the leather notebook on the table. "It's a journal Ransom kept when he was at Harrison."

He was King Arthur, dying and old, and I was faithful Galahad, presenting the Grail. Joel just stared at it, silent and motionless.

"Ransom was always writing in it. I can't tell you how many times I saw him off in the distance somewhere writing in that book. I was looking for it, actually, that morning I saw you in the hallway. I found it one night, about a month later, when I was browsing through the Salinger shelf in the library. I think he knew I would find it eventually."

Joel hunched over his son's solitary creation, not touching it yet.

"I spent the past three weeks reading it with another friend of his—his only other friend, really. Her name's Maggie. Sorry it took me so long to get it to you, Joel. It was selfish of me. I just wasn't thinking."

"It's okay, Fin," he said. "Would you mind leaving me alone for a while?"

"Of course not," I replied.

Three hours and six coffee refills later, my hands were shaking. As I sat, attempting to read, Joel entered into the living room and tossed a folded envelope onto the sofa.

"This was waiting in the mail when I got back from Harrison," he said. "You can read it if you like."

I knew what it was, of course. I'd known when I first asked Mr. Seaborn if I could visit. I'd known since the moment I first found the journal. It was Ransom's last page, his suicide note. Trembling, I pulled it from the envelope, held the well-worn, familiar paper, and read.

September 21
Today's the day, same as her. I sat on a bench as the sun

rose in the east, and saw my fate with blistering clarity. My fate, my purpose, my calling. And she sat beside me, a dim, wayward angel, a banged up road sign. And I'm thinking of my father, another angel, of sorts, though unsung and under appreciated. I'm thinking of my father, and the world I leave behind to him, a world made brighter by my passing.

Here's my secret, Dad. I killed her just as if I'd shot her with this gun. Every other day I'd rush home knowing she'd awaken from her nap thirsty for wine, hungry for pills. Every other day I'd yell idiotic questions through the bathroom door and rush in whenever she stopped answering. Every other day I was her guardian angel, her brave little infidel. Not that day. I walked slowly and told myself over and over this was mercy, she'd had enough, she was ready to fly. I got home and didn't call to her or run to her or even look at the bathroom door. I left her there, withering, to die. Then I found a poem this summer, a poem she'd written that week, that fucking week, the last fucking week of her life and I knew how wrong I'd been, how badly I'd misread her. She wanted to live, Daddy. She wasn't ready to leave us. She still needed me to protect her from herself. She still needed me. I killed her. I killed my mom. I killed your wife. I killed her.

The Promise of Autumn by Rosemary Gardner

Summer passes, swift moving current
The flowers wither, dying.
In shining colorscapes we only
Feign joyfulness.
The dark of nightfall thickens
Denser, ever, 'till midnight
And masks the Oak branch heavy with
Mosquito blood.

None are spared the promise of Autumn.
The Blue Jay takes up lodging
Elsewhere.
While we remain suffering
The aftermath

I'm sorry to hurt you Dad. I know how you tried.

I am the blade of grass, and winter is eternal, and God is the cloud-covered sun, and life is the snow that buries and numbs me. I see no point to remaining.

The words literally knocked the wind out of me. I don't know what it was, but in that moment I felt the overwhelming sadness he had carried with him always and the weariness of his ceaseless battle. I looked up at Joel, but could hardly see him through my tears.

❦

Our footsteps squeaked in the snow as we traversed the cemetery ground. We stood between the graves of his son and wife. Sun poked through the afternoon clouds, making a late-day appearance before nightfall. Side by side, the head stones sent a chill through me. Their dedications were simple: Beloved Son. Beloved Wife, Mother and Poet.

"He carried that enormous weight all by himself," Joel said. "All his life he thought he was her protector. It took all his energy and focus. That's why he didn't talk to anyone, he was too absorbed in his mission…his job.

"And I didn't really know how far gone she was," he continued. "I thought I knew. I pretended I knew. But I didn't know. Only Ransom knew. That's my life's biggest failing: not knowing what he knew; not forcing that weight off his shoulders. That's what I have to live with."

"I think he loved you very much," I said. "It almost seems like he was embarrassed to show love. But I really think he loved you."

Suddenly I was crying again, gentle, peaceful tears that surprised me, as did my deep desire to comfort this sad, good man.

"Thanks for saying that, Finbar. That means a lot to me. I loved him, too."

Then I realized I wasn't crying alone.

❦

He cooked a chicken and rice dinner. Afterwards, he boiled us water for tea.

"So, tell me about Maggie," he said.

"She had it pretty bad for Ransom," I began. "She was in his poetry class when he was a sophomore. One day, he recited a poem your wife had written, and Maggie got curious. She followed him after class, and they became friends. It never got far beyond that, mostly because Ransom couldn't handle it."

"What's she like?" he asked.

"Well, first of all, she's just kind. One of those people who are somehow singled out to be kinder, and gentler, and more sympathetic. And she's pretty, and smart and everything. And she has a great sense of humor."

"Can she juggle?"

"I wouldn't be surprised," I responded. "To be honest with you, I wanted to talk with you about Maggie." He had become my therapist, my confessor, and I didn't get the feeling he minded. He, too, existed on that higher plane. "I've kind of fallen in love with her, Joel. Do you think there's anything wrong with that?"

I was asking him to speak on behalf of his son, a proxy approval. Did I have Ransom's blessing?

"Listen, Fin, it's been my experience that real love doesn't come along very often, and it's almost never wrong to chase it when you find it. If Ransom was alive, and the two of them were going steady, I'd say there was a problem. But as it stands, you're in the clear."

"It just feels strange," I continued, "I mean, we were both friends with Ransom, and it was his death that brought us together. I sometimes feel like he's with us, watching us. Does that sound crazy?"

"No, Fin, it doesn't sound crazy at all. Maybe he is with you sometimes. If he is, I'm sure he's happy that he led you to each other. Maybe he feels like it's his life's crowning achievement. You have our blessing."

He smiled, knowing how much it meant to me.

"Can I ask you a personal question, Joel?"

"Sure," he replied.

"What did Ransom mean in the journal when he talked about a younger brother?"

"Rosemary got pregnant right after we moved here," he said. "Ransom was three. I don't know how he knew about it. Maybe there was a sense of loss surrounding us for a while. Hell, maybe it never went away. Maybe she talked about it to him.

"We wanted that baby, Finbar. I wanted that baby. But Rosemary was getting worse and she couldn't handle the strain. She became suicidal. At the time it seemed to come down to either losing the baby, or losing Rosemary and the baby. It broke my heart. It broke Rosemary's heart, too. I don't think she ever really got over it. More nights than I can remember I found her sitting on the porch or in the den rocking our imaginary child."

We went on like that for hours, meandering between easy

and difficult subjects, talking like he and Ransom never could, never would. For a few hours, I was his son and he was my friend. At one point near the end of the night he asked, "Do you believe in God, Fin?"

I laughed. "That's exactly what I asked Ransom once."

"I know," he said. "I read the journal, remember? I guess what I'm asking is how do you picture God? Can you define Him...or Her?"

I thought for a moment, wanting to come through with some sparkling gem of wisdom, but he spoke again before I could answer.

"Let me tell you what I think," he said. "And this is kind of how I survive all that happened. I remember how I felt about Ransom from the very first moment I laid eyes on him. I mean I thought I knew what love was before then, but it was nothing like what I felt for him. And in that moment, when he was just a newborn baby I already forgave him for anything wrong he would ever do in his life. Anything," he emphasized. "I loved him unconditionally. Imagine how God loves us. I mean I'm just a weak, struggling human being and I could honestly have forgiven Ransom anything you could imagine, any sin at all. Multiply that by about a thousand. That's God."

🍁

I awakened before dawn. My bus was scheduled to depart at six. Joel was in the living room when I emerged.

"Morning, Fin," he said. I wondered if he'd even slept.

"Morning, Joel," I answered.

"Before you take off, there's something I want to show you."

He led me to a door that opened into the garage. Inside sat Ransom's '72 Scamp. Joel always parked his Suburban in the driveway. Now I knew why.

"I want you to have it," he said, not giving me a chance to respond. "I even got it tuned up for you. You shouldn't have any trouble making it back to Pittsburgh, or Pembrook, or wherever you're going."

"I don't know what to say," I remarked, dumbfounded.

"Just say you'll take it. I'm sure he would have wanted you to have it."

"Thank you."

As we shook hands, he pulled me toward him. We embraced.

"I'm really glad you came, Finbar."

"Me too."

The Scamp had surprising power and it took me awhile to get used to it's quick acceleration. It wasn't like I didn't have time, though—thirteen hours to Pembrook.

I listened to talk shows on the AM radio and bits of football games as I picked them up. I felt good. I remembered Ransom sitting where I sat, drinking beer, not saying a word. I was glad I had known him. Once I hit Pennsylvania, I stopped in a rest area to make a call.

"Dad, it's Dan," I said, shutting out the sounds of motors and laughter.

"Where are you, Dan?"

I explained that Mr. Seaborn had given me Ransom's car and that I was over half way home. "I think I'm just gonna go straight to school," I said. "I can pick up my laundry next weekend."

"How'd it go, Dan? Did you find what you were looking for?"

"Yeah, Dad, I think so. Thanks for letting me go."

I was smiling.

❧

I continued my journey along the interstates. It wouldn't be long now before I arrived. I thought of the many sad days that had filled my recent months and decided each one had been worth it, worth this sweet feeling of knowing she was there, and that soon I would be with her.

I'd tell her the story of Joel Seaborn and of Ransom's missing last page. I'd recall as vividly as I could my trip to the river, my early lunch in Hanover, our visit to the gravesite, his gift of Ransom's automobile and the long drive home. I'd kiss her mouth and face and hold tightly this woman who had helped me toe the fine line between life and death, and lifted me to her. I'd whisper again and again, for as long as I could, for as long as she would listen, "I love you, Maggie."

❧

There's a gun on the table. It's loaded. It was surprisingly easy to obtain. An AA friend put me in touch with the right people. It's amazing what folks will do for you when they trust you.

I hold it in my hands for at least an hour every day. I'm surprised by how good it feels...how much like a natural extension.

Me, with a gun, at a table, in a dingy motel—how did I get here?

Chapter Eleven

The remainder of that school year was like a dream; one from which you never want to awaken. Though the difference in our ages drew some attention in the Harrison fish bowl, the bond of our journey made us immune. Eventually we just became part of the scenery, the lovesick couple that could be found at any hour talking on benches, kissing in corners, walking along sidewalks. I can still remember what it felt like being near her then—the sense I carried of having been chosen, of my heart possessing a living, breathing treasure in the form of her presence.

Things changed, of course, with graduation. Maggie and Jessica followed through with their plan and spent the summer hiking through Europe. In a series of postcards I was kept abreast of their every move and assured of the fact that I was deeply missed, at least by one of them. Youth, time, and distance combined to form the seed of doubt in me, though— sensing the turn that would have to come. I knew she was fading. I would lose her. We were doomed.

It went like this:

"I love you, Finbar."

"I love you, too, Maggie."

The lump was already there in my throat—a psychic signal. Here it was. The moment I'd been living in my head every minute of every day, pretty much.

"But we have to be realistic here." We were on the steps of St. Augustine's, her first visit since returning to America. A sidewalk light encircled us as we sat in the presence of my pending emptiness. "You have three more years of school, Fin. That's a long time. And I'll be trying to find my way out in the world."

"I really don't like where this is going, Maggie," I said, my voice like a thin piece of paper in the wind.

"I don't like it either, Fin, but we have to be realistic."

She was crying.

"Yeah, you said that," I replied.

"Don't you dare be mean, Finbar," she said. "If you don't know how hard this is for me then you don't really know me."

Her sniffles and the humming engines of cars driving in the distance filled the pause that followed. By some gift of grace, perhaps emanating from the giant church behind us, I crawled through the muck of my baser instincts and clawed my way to higher ground, seeing her clearly in that moment, trusting her anguish and knowing that it mirrored mine identically almost and that in the end, she was right about where we were and what we had to do.

"I'm sorry, Maggie," I said. "It's just that I don't feel like I can stop loving you or wanting to be with you just because you say it's realistic."

"I still want to be with you, too, Fin. And if we're meant to be together we will be. But in the meantime we won't put so much pressure on ourselves. Does that make sense?"

"So what are you saying exactly? We see other people?"

"If we feel like it," she replied, a faint lightness returning.

"And then we pick up where we left off and live happily ever after."

But that's never the way it goes, is it? We tell ourselves we're doing things for the right reasons, even when we're not totally sure, and those decisions lead us to other ones and we're suddenly on a completely different path.

❧

Upon my return to Harrison the following August I began to cultivate a new role, quite different from the happy one I'd perfected with my co-star Maggie the previous semester. I'll call it: The Tortured Artist. I wrote very serious songs. I smoked cigarettes and bonded with other expatriates (some of whom were in The *Star Trek* gang.) I resumed my late-night strolls.

Maggie visited just once—in early October, Homecoming weekend. We went out to dinner. We sat through a movie. We walked the same pathways we'd walked a hundred times before. But our forced, grown-up neutrality stood in such sharp contrast to the gushing bliss of our previous time spent there, it pierced a hole in my heart. We kissed and we laughed and we even made some vague plans, but the next afternoon's good-bye felt dangerously permanent. It left a sour taste that could only be erased with hard liquor.

Did I mention the drinking?

❧

The remainder of my college years would see me graduate from the ranks of amateur weekend pleasure seeker to aspiring professional. I sought out others inclined to excess and we made a hobby of our exploits: champagne before Chapel, the Landmark for an early lunch, final exams taken while bombed. When any one became tired of the life, there was always another to take his place, another drinking buddy to be found. Some days I went through as many as three drink-vomit cycles. But I was a college kid, protected by my carefree station, beyond reproach.

At some point my semi-regular calls to check in with Maggie transformed into late-night drunken word-odysseys, the content, on my end at least, wavering like jazz between meanness, love and naked pleading. By the end, she was begging me not to call. And some time, maybe two years later, I complied.

※

Graduation did not represent an increase in responsibility. A musician's life is every bit as conducive to lechery and alcohol abuse as a student's. You're encouraged to get drunk, sleep around, be a loud-mouthed idiot. That's how you make a name for yourself. During that time, it was common for me to awaken in a strange bed, in a strange room, with troubling fragments of the previous night pulsing through my head, keeping the beat of my brain-splitting hangovers.

"Did we have sex?"

"How did we get here?"

The answers never came.

※

Sundays. That's where the real trouble started. I'd find myself at a friend's house for a Steelers game or a rented movie, drinking wine or the beer left over from the party we'd had the night before. Hair of the dog. Finbar the wild man. Eventually, somebody would drive me home and I'd be every bit as plastered as I'd been the night before.

Sundays turned into Mondays and Mondays into Tuesdays. Before I knew it, every single day of the week began with the consumption of a six-pack, the breakfast of champions. The beer will keep me steady, I thought. The beer will keep the world from knowing how drunk I was last night. It got to where I couldn't remember going to whichever part-time job I hadn't lost yet. It got to where my friends and family had long talks with me and stopped drinking or serving alcohol in my presence. It got to where I finally found my bottom.

It was a balmy spring night. A Saturday. Eric Sebastian's wedding was at noon. I drank on the way. At the reception, I slow danced with Mrs. Clark, my drunken erection rubbing against her fleshy thigh. I pissed into a plant holder. I did shots with each member of the wedding party individually. I made a pass at Mike Imuso's new girlfriend. When the party died down I drove to a bar in Oakland, where I crashed the set of a friend's band, knocking instruments from stands, and singing off key at the top of my lungs into the lead singer's microphone.

I remember searching for my car and being ecstatic when I finally found it. I remember racing along the streets of Pittsburgh, singing along with the radio. I remember flying through the Fort Pitt Tunnels, scanning stations, passing cars effortlessly. I remember the speedometer getting up over ninety, nosing up toward one hundred. I remember bumping gently against a cement barrier and coming to on a stretcher…traffic passing slowly in a single lane.

"Did anyone die?" I asked the paramedic. "Did I kill anybody?"

"Nobody died," he said. "But you sure as hell should have."

"Can somebody help me please? I think I need some help."

❧

I attended my first AA meeting two weeks later. The district court gave me no choice in the matter.

A biker who called himself 'Slick Willie' told a story about his childhood on the North Side. A chill ran the length of my spine as I listened to his story and saw myself in every word. It was my face in the cracked bathroom mirror he described, my temper flaring from the whiskey, my spirit crippled by unexplainable fear. Tears of recognition poured from my eyes. I stood at the hour's conclusion and introduced myself.

❧

Erie was one of the band's regular stops. We played at a club called Alley Cats, a long, thin hole in the wall on Fleet Street. By our third visit, we had local media interested. A newspaper interviewed me over the phone and ran a story previewing our Friday night show.

The band had jelled into a tight unit over the past several months. The packed house, a sea of faces at my feet, devoured every song.

She sat at the bar. Our eyes finally met near the end of the first set as we covered the Van Morrison song, *Sweet Thing*. I nearly forgot the words. On the break, I waded through the crowd until I stood beside her.

"Maggie," I said, trying to contain my excitement, "what are you doing here?"

"I read about it in the paper. You're famous." She smiled and stood to hug me. "How are you doing, Finbar? God, it's been a long time."

"I'm doing pretty well," I replied.

"I see that," she said, waving her beer at the crowd.

"How about you? What's going on with you?"

"I'm living with my Dad and Charlene," she explained.

"I stayed in Dayton until last year teaching at an elementary school. But then I broke up with the guy I'd been seeing and decided there was no reason to stay there any longer. I'm a substitute in the Erie public school system for now. I'm lucky if I work three days a week. You need a beer?"

"No, I don't drink any more," I replied with the quiet satisfaction I'd felt more often since getting sober. "Man, you look good, Maggie. It doesn't seem fair that you've gotten prettier and I've stayed the same."

I was laying on the old Finbar charm. She blushed.

"What else?" she asked. "Tell me everything."

"There isn't that much to tell, Maggie. After I graduated I moved back to Pittsburgh and found part time jobs. I kept writing songs, and playing them for people whenever I could. I finally hooked up with these guys last March. We're doing really well, especially in Pittsburgh. There's a song about you on our CD," I confessed.

"Oh yeah?" she said. "I hope you weren't too mean."

"It's not mean, Maggie. I'm just kind of a slow healer," I said, letting the words float through the air. "I'm sorry, by the way, for what an idiot I was after we broke up."

"I'm sorry for a lot of things, Fin," she replied.

Then it was her words floating through the air.

The second set was even better than the first. I was inspired by her presence. When we were done, she waited around as we loaded our gear out the back door. Standing on the sidewalk outside the club, she scribbled her number on the back of a matchbook and I promised to call.

❧

We talked for three hours that Monday filling in our respective missing years: the gigs I'd played, the places I'd been, and her life as a teacher, the boyfriends who'd come and gone. The old chemistry instantly returned, and fires burned anew in me, fires I'd pissed on for the last half decade but whose flames I'd never properly extinguished.

"Are you happy, Finbar?" she asked in a phone call some weeks later.

"I'm getting there," I replied.

❧

She received an offer from a high school in Pittsburgh to work as a guidance counselor. She found an apartment on a cobblestone street, not far from my parents, not far from me.

We were a couple again, only grown up now. Instead of in a cluttered dorm room, we passed our time in her cluttered living room. Instead of the Harrison sidewalks, we walked beside the Allegheny River. Instead of our next exams, we talked about her students, my band, our future.

❧

Christmas Eve morning I awakened before her. She'd be leaving for Erie in a few hours to celebrate the holiday with her family. Quietly, I tiptoed out of the bedroom and went to retrieve my guitar, which I'd brought with me the night before.

"Maggie," I whispered, nudging her gently. "Can I give you a special Christmas Eve concert before you go?"

"Sure." She smiled, yawning, not all the way awake yet, and turned onto her side. I launched into a quiet song I had composed specifically for the occasion, *Distant Thunder*.

I can see your daddy's worried
That I won't take care of you
'cause I ain't got no steady income

No realistic point of view
Don't he know that heaven smiles on
Those who live the life they love
That's why you hear the sound of
distant thunder, coming from above....

After I'd finished, I reached into my guitar case and pulled out the small velvet box. I opened it and handed it to her.

"I love you, Maggie," I said, kneeling as if in prayer. "Will you marry me?"

Once the color had returned to her cheeks, she answered, "I would love to be your wife."

❦

I'd call her from every rest stop when we toured.

"What's going on?"

"I went to dinner with your folks last night. How was the gig?"

"Not too bad. The radio station pushed it pretty hard."

"Any news from RCA?"

"The usual; they're reissuing the single in a few weeks. You never know."

"I miss you, Fin."

"I miss you, too, Maggie. I'll be home Sunday."

"I can't wait."

❦

"Are we still newlyweds?" I asked, laying beside her on a Sunday morning, my hand tickling the skin of her bare thigh.

"No," she answered, "we've been married almost fifteen months. You're only newlyweds for the first year."

She nibbled at my neck and I shivered.

"So we're no longer newlyweds?" I clarified, easing my hand under her short silk nightie.

"No," she murmured, concentrating now on my left shoulder. "We're no longer newlyweds."

"Well, I don't see much point in staying married then," I countered, pulling her on top of me. "The romance is obviously gone."

"I'll call my attorney in the morning," she said.

※

Her period was late by three days, which wasn't unusual, but still, late. We hadn't planned on her getting pregnant, but the idea appealed to us. On a whim, I ran out to the nearest drug store and bought a home pregnancy test. After she'd administered it privately in the bathroom, we set the plastic gizmo on the dresser and retreated to the bed.

"What are we doing this for?" she asked. "There's no way I'm pregnant. We've been careful, haven't we?"

"Not really," I answered.

"There's no way I'm pregnant." She giggled, imagining for a second that she was wrong.

"Is it time yet?" I asked.

We were children at the top of the stairs on Christmas morning. Try as we might, we couldn't curb our hopes or quell the feeling that something momentous was occurring.

"You check," she said. "I'm too nervous."

"Let's look together."

We approached gingerly, as if it might run away if we frightened it.

"I can't look, Fin. Just tell me."

She ran back onto the bed. I froze in my tracks, seeing the

solid vertical line through the chalk-white circle. We'd known it all along.

"We're going to have a baby," I said. "We're going to have a baby."

We lived the next nine months in dazed bliss.

❋

I awakened in a hotel room. My band roommate on the road was the guitar player, Dave who slept peacefully on the other double bed. I grabbed my jeans and snuck down to the lobby to call Maggie on my cell. She answered on the first ring.

"Hey."

"Hey."

"How did it go last night?"

We'd played a club in Cincinnati—a town we had never quite been able to crack.

"Great," I fibbed. In truth, we were losing steam since the label had decided to place its attention on every band but ours. "It's a little hard concentrating, though, when I know my wife might be going into labor at any moment. How are you feeling?"

"I feel great...other than the whole beached whale thing." I literally ached to be sitting beside her right then. "I think I'll be able to hold off 'til you come home. But I don't think I'll make it much past that."

"Well don't forget my handy dandy pager," I said. "I've been wearing it on my belt each night. It props my guitar up nicely."

We agreed that she would call it the moment anything happened, even if she knew we were mid-set.

I saw a movie.

I called Maggie.

I bought a new novel and tried to start reading it.

I called Maggie.

I people watched. Chicago is a great city for that.

I called Maggie.

Finally, at 3, it was time for us to load our gear into the venue. We sound-checked, ate dinner, waited in the dressing room. It became a running joke for members of the band to suggest I check in with Maggie.

I called Maggie.

❧

During the last song of our set, the pager went off on my belt. I made a joke to the audience before running off stage and calling Maggie as the band and crew went into swat-team mode.

"It's happening, Fin," she said through the long-distance phone-line. "The contractions just started."

"Oh my God."

"Dr. Stetman said it will be a while…probably not 'till late this morning. I'll make sure to wait until you're here, Fin."

"Oh my God, Maggie…"

"Just be careful. Please be careful. Everything will be all right."

"Isn't that my line?" I asked.

"I love you, Finbar."

"I love you too, Maggie."

She died before I made it home.

❧

The roads are a sheet of ice. I don't know how the hell I made it here without crashing.

Pete almost seemed to recognize me when I went up to the bar just now. I swear a smile like that of an old friend's began creeping across his nearly toothless mouth.

"Merry Christmas Eve," he said. "What can I get for you?"

"A beer and a shot," I replied. "Budweiser. Beam."

It was one of those slow motion moments. I imagined the whole bar—four, late afternoon, holiday drinkers, Pete's cronies, watching me as I walked back to my table, sensing the significance of the event. I lifted the wet, rust-brown bottle to my lips. With one sip, five years of sobriety were washed away.

The clock radio went off at five o'clock in the afternoon. Bob Dylan's voice filled the dark motel room. I smelled the clothes I still wore, saturated with bar smoke, and nearly gagged. I held a loaded Smith & Wesson revolver in my right hand but was still breathing. I must have passed out. I placed the gun gently on the bed, stood, grabbed my coat, and walked out of room 29.

I walked and I walked without thinking and covered the distance to town. A thick snow fell, covering my face and coat. On Main Street everything was closed for Christmas.

I turned right on Elm and found the path that led up to Harrison, my first time back in twelve years. I stood at the bottom of the ageless quadrangle, the vast, white rectangle with the clock tower head. The snow fell harder, obstructing my vision, cooling my face. I remembered standing in that exact spot, the first week of my first year, feeling so small and alone.

Roaming the campus, I saw him again, walking hunched on the narrow sidewalks, writing like mad at his library desk, opening the door to his room in Jefferson, a cigarette hanging from his lips. Always, he carried the weathered brown journal, our window, at last, to his soul.

With Ransom came Maggie, of course. The sweet girl from long ago touching my arm in the chapel, lifting me off of the parking lot ground, sitting across from me night after night. In a precious and crystalline moment, I knew what I'd come there to find. Not a solitary end, like my long forgotten friend, but the memory of Maggie, as she appeared then, the shining counterpoint to Ransom's dark longings. Her love, like mercy, returned to me.

There are those of us strugglers who see the light before it is too late. And there are those of us who don't.

I retraced my steps through Harrison, through town. My Jeep stood sideways in the middle of the otherwise deserted parking lot. Lazy-eyed Lou waved sadly through the office window.

"Merry Christmas," he mouthed.

I climbed inside and headed for Pittsburgh, to tell you the story of how I met your mother.

Bill Deasy is an accomplished songwriter and recording artist. When he's not traveling the globe in support of his music, he lives with his wife and family in Pittsburgh, Pennsylvania.

Ransom Seaborn is his first novel.

The author would like to thank all those who read this book along the way—you know who you are. He would also like to thank the talented staff at Velluminous Press for taking such good care.

Printed in the United States
59041LVS00001B/64

9 781905 605088